My Father Took A Cake To France

Cynthia Flood

Talonbooks • Vancouver • 1992

Copyright © 1992 Cynthia Flood

Published with the assistance of the Canada Council

Talonbooks
201-1019 E. Cordova
Vancouver, British Columbia,
Canada V6A 1M8

Designed by Penny Goldsmith, typeset in Bem 11/13 by
Pièce de Résistance Ltée., and printed and bound in Canada
by Hignell Printing Ltd.

First printing July 1992

Some of these stories have appeared, in slightly different form,
in the following periodicals and anthologies: *The Malahat
Review, Books in Canada, Room of One's Own, Quarry, Descant,
Frictions: Stories by Women,* and *The Journey Prize Anthology.*

Canadian Cataloguing in Publication Data

    Flood, Cynthia, 1940–
      My father took a cake to France

    ISBN 0-88922-310-6

    I. Title.
    PS8561.L64M9 1992   C813'.54   C92-091271-0
    PR9199.3.F56M9 1992

for Dean
with thanks for all the flowers

Contents

The Meaning of the Marriage

Mrs. Perren marries my grandfather on a Tuesday afternoon, late, so providing a wedding meal is unnecessary. The guests simply drink tea and eat pound cake. On the Tuesday morning, Mrs. Perren comes with her sister to inspect my grandfather's house. (I don't know where he is.) They find everything very clean. The oak floors shine, as do the thin high windows. Mrs. Perren's sister is enthusiastic about a man who keeps house so. (My grandfather is a saddler.) The two women see the bedroom prepared for the motherless little girl, my mother, who is now to leave her grandparents' house and come to live with her father, because he will again have a wife.

The sisters end their tour in the kitchen. Glass-fronted cupboards go right up to the ceiling, so Mrs. Perren stands on a chair to inspect the topmost shelves. From her altitude she sees out to the back yard, where a nasty box-headed tomcat rolls about in the sun-dappled shade of the maple. She sends the sister out with a broom. Then the two leave my grandfather's house to go along to the village dressmaker.

During the many fittings of her wedding dress, the bride has been narrowly inspected, for she is not local; this unknown woman is to replace my dead grandmother and to "take on" my mother, aged five. Mrs. Perren's wedding garment is of mauve silk, for she has been a widow long enough to finish with black and dove-grey in their turn. The dress is the bride's "best" for some time after the ceremony; it moves then through a sequence of annual demotions which lead to temporary burial in the rag bag, but thence it rises to magnificent resurrection in the crazy quilt on the spare room bed. Mrs. Perren was a notable quilter.

Of the rite I know only that it was Methodist, though Mrs. Perren, I believe, adhered to a harder covenant. I don't know if my mother was at the wedding, to carry flowers for her new step-mother. At the little reception, did she chatter and clown to get the attention she was accustomed to? How did my grandfather feel on his wedding night? He was after all a veteran. His first wife had died after childbirth, taking twin girls with her to the grave, and his second, my grandmother, proved no more durable. A beautiful twenty-six, she fell victim to the same "childbed fever" as her predecessor . . . but her offspring survived.

Looking at my grandmother's photograph, taken in the year of her marriage and death, made me feel strange when I turned twenty-six. Years later I told my mother so. For her, she said, the strangest time had been when she herself was fifty-two. These jumping years unnerve me. Two days after my first daughter's birth, my body's temperature rose. I lay cold and sweating, could not eat, wept feebly on the nurse when she arrived at last. *Chills, headache, malaise, and anorexia are common.* In no time flat I was out of the ward, into isolation, on antibiotics. *Treatment consists of debridement by curettage and administration of penicillin*; I don't remember being debrided. The baby ran a fever too. Nobody named the poison in us.

Could my grandmother's family bring themselves to attend the wedding? My great-grandmother did make the pound cake for the occasion. I know, because over the years Mrs. Perren was repeatedly plaintive to her new husband and his little girl about its impropriety: "A fruit-cake would have been seemlier." Perhaps Mrs. Perren felt that the rite hadn't really "taken."

How did my great-grandmother feel as she mixed the butter and sugar and flour, a pound of each? And did she and my great-grandfather witness the wedding that featured the same bridegroom as in their daughter's ceremony and was held in the same church? There also my grandmother's funeral had been conducted, with, as my mother always says, "the entire village in tears." This is a direct quotation from my great-grandparents, who told and retold to my mother the terrible story of their daughter's death. The narrative shaped the ends of their lives. My great-grandparents also told my mother, repeatedly, that their dead daughter was a joyful woman. My mother still repeats this to me. Her voice lingers with the phrasing. "My mother made everyone laugh with her," she says. The pound cake suggests that my great-grandmother tried to wish the new marriage well (not perhaps so well as to merit candied fruit).

That is all I have for the story's opening.

Next comes a story set in the same polished kitchen that Mrs. Perren and her sister saw on the wedding morning. (I never heard a thing else about that sister.)

My mother is now nine, and wears a green checked dress. Her dark hair shines and her eyes are hazel like mine, like her dead mother's. Her cheeks are hot. In her hands is a small box, dark blue leather. The clasp is stiff, my mother's fingers determined, and the opening lid reveals a set of miniature ivory-handled cutlery. Oh perfect, she sees, for raspberries on leaf plates with girlfriends in the back yard, for imaginary cat-banquets with the strays watching lickerishly from the lower branches of the maple . . . . The little things exactly fit her hands. (My mother now looks with disbelief at her arthritic digits.)

Who has given her this present? Its extravagance suggests grandparents. My mother has never said. I don't think she cares. The cutlery's fate is far more important than its provenance. My step-grandmother snatches the box away. She throws it into the wood stove. With the toasting fork, she rams the gift well down into the flames. "Sinful waste," says Mrs. Perren, "and for a wicked girl like you." Burning leather smells dreadful.

Why didn't my grandfather stop her? He isn't there, in the story.

Then did my mother tell him, crying, when he came home from work? Why didn't he do something then? Or later?

Mrs. Perren did not approve of pets—I believe she was originally a farm woman—and so my mother played with the neighbours' cats and dogs, and with strays. Mrs. Perren said they were all "dirty beasts." One such was the box-headed tomcat, which turned out to have been a female rolling about desirously in heat; Tipsy's kittens caused the first full confrontation between step-mother and step-daughter. Yet my mother has always been vague about this story, never releasing details about how "she got rid of them." When—rarely—she talks about her step-mother, she usually tells about the poison.

This story begins in an act of straightforward evil: Some person or persons unknown leave gobbets of raw meat daubed with strychnine up and down the village lanes. Dying cats and dogs writhe and yowl and froth. Now thirteen years old, my mother is frantic to hold the dying animals, stroke, comfort. Not unreasonably (in her narrative, my mother is always careful so to characterize the action), my step-grandmother refuses permission.

What Mrs. Perren does instead is to walk my mother out to the back lane and hold her there, forcibly, to watch one of the cats complete its death. She does this to convey to my mother the meaning of the expression "tortures of the damned," for, as Mrs. Perren says to the thirteen-year-old girl, "You do not know yet that you are wicked, and it is my business to teach you."

I can never bear this part, and break in. "But your father, why didn't he do something so she wouldn't be so mean to you?"

The answer never satisfies. "Well," my mother says mildly, "*she* was looking after me, you know. I was her job. And everybody said I was very spoiled. My grandparents—they were broken-hearted, you see. I looked exactly like my mother. My step-mother probably told my father I was difficult. I suppose I was. And he was a quiet man."

A twenty-year gap comes between this story and the next. My mother, thirty-three years old and now really a mother, drives out from Toronto to the village with her little son, my older brother. She drives out on a pretty spring day to visit my step-grandmother. Why?

Mrs. Perren is a widow again. My grandfather died when my mother was twenty-six.

Why does my mother, fully-orphaned now, make this journey?

I still think of Mrs. Perren as Mrs. Perren; she doesn't feel like a relative. Recently, it came to me that I don't even know her first name. She must have come *from somewhere* when she and her sister walked up to that thin clean house on that Tuesday. What happened to Mr. Perren? Why were there no little Perrens? Why did she remarry, at forty? My grandfather presumably sought the stability of husband-hood and of having a mother-substitute for his child; losing *this* wife to puerperal fever was unlikely. If age was one of Mrs. Perren's charms, what were those of a middle-aged saddler with two dead wives and a young wilful child? What were her options?

My mother drives out to see her step-mother.

All I know of my step-grandmother, this woman who has so influenced my own life and my brother's, lies in these stories and questions. I tack them together into the rough shape of Mrs. Perren's ignorance and hate; as a dress for the tale, they suffice. But *he* is missing. The man is missing—my grandfather. Where is he? I do not know one single story about him. The space where he should be is a blatant absence that magnetizes me.

My mother tells me about my *great*-grandfather, about a time when he goes to England, I don't know why. While there, he makes a purchase for my great-grandmother and her five sisters: beautiful silk. (Every decent woman must have her good black dress.) To get the goods past Canadian customs, my great-grandfather wraps the gleaming yardage around his waist and so passes, unscathed though bulky, under authority's eye. This story, pleasingly, takes the edge off the intimidating probity of my forbears. I like to imagine my great-grandfather in his stateroom as the ship pulls in to Quebec, breathing heavily, winding the stuff round and round himself and pinning it firmly at his sides. Further back, I like to see him in the English shop— in London? in a textile city of the Midlands?—looking at the black shining rivers of fabric. "Yes, this is good. Rachel will like this."

Those sisters—my great-great-aunts, are they?—I know stories about them too. One has a daughter, Sarah, who dithers in her selection of a husband until my great-great-aunt loses patience and declares, "Sarah! You will go round and round the bush and choose a crooked stick at last!" I even know that Sarah's marriage in fact turns out well. And I know that another great-great-aunt, designated to teach my mother tatting, finally takes away from her the small circle of grubby botched work and issues the verdict: "Some are not born to tat."

But I have not even a little story like these about my grandfather.

Mrs. Perren did not like the story about the smuggled silk. (In what context did she hear it?) My mother says simply, "My step-mother disapproved." Of the purchase itself? Of the deceit? Yet she used strips of that silk to edge the splendid crazy quilt she created for the spare room in my grandfather's house. How did the scraps get to Mrs. Perren? Perhaps my great-grandmother and great-great-aunts sent them along as a compliment, intended to soften; competent needlewomen themselves, they recognized, but did not possess, the talent required to conceive such an extraordinary bedcovering as my mother describes. To follow a pattern—log-cabin or wedding ring or Texas star—is one thing; to create *ex nihilo*, quite another. Buying material would be dreadful waste. No. The quilt-maker must use whatever has come to her rag bag through the years, and thence generate a design that exploits those random colours and textures, displays them to their utmost brilliance. Thus she is midwife to a metamorphosis. In her quilt, the scraps and bits and tatters fuse and then explode into a shapely galaxy of shattered stained glass.

Perhaps my great-grandmother and my great-great-aunts hoped, through this gift, to win influence over Mrs. Perren, to move her towards a gentler treatment of my mother. They must have mourned to see the little girl, beloved both for her resemblance to the dead and for her own living sweetness and dearness, unhappily exiled in that mother-loveless dwelling. But perhaps I'm just making up that supposition; perhaps none of them even knew how my mother felt—my mother, another scrap sent from house to house. Did she ever speak of her misery, then? I don't know—but for those women I can imagine possibilities, scenes, expressions. My grandfather's face I cannot see.

So now my mother is thirty-three. Her visit to Mrs. Perren may be intended to say, "You taught me I was evil. You did all you could to stop me from living my life, yet I have won. I am educated, a trained teacher. I have travelled. I am married, pretty, happy. I have borne a beautiful healthy son." The subtext is clear: "None of this is true of you, step-mother." Yet that is not the story she tells of the visit.

She only told me the full story once, when I was young. Now my mother wants me to tell her how the story ends.

During the visit, my brother is noisily vigorous, running about the neat back yard and stomping in the kitchen and wanting to throw his ball in the livingroom.

Mrs. Perren says to my mother, "Take him away."

My mother is angry, but she does not leave. Instead she leads my brother upstairs, to show him mummy's room when she was a little girl. Mrs. Perren does not go upstairs any more (arthritis), has not for some years; a bed has been placed for her in the dining room. So she sits, alone again, in the chair by the window. How does she pass the time today, any day? She can no longer quilt. No novels—devil's work. Perhaps Mrs. Perren reads the Bible, looks out the window and disapproves of passersby.

I can imagine thus about my step-grandmother, my great-grandfather, my great-great-aunts. I cannot imagine about my grandfather, because my imagination requires a toehold on the known world, and I know no stories about him.

Up the stairs go my mother and my brother, in the story, and as they climb they smell the musty acrid odour of stale cat excrement, stronger and stronger, nearer and nearer. In the spare room, a branch, from the maple tree beloved in my mother's youth, has pierced the window. The wind has shaken out big shards of glass, the tree has kept on growing, and now a convenient cat-bridge leads to shelter and relative warmth. Right now, as my mother and brother enter the room, they find two animals dozing on the quilt. Silk and velveteen and grosgrain and muslin and polished cotton and gingham and corduroy and chintz, triangles and rhomboids and squares in all the colours—all are smeared, all stained, rumpled. Cat fur lies thick. A drift floats, airborne, as one cat rushes out the broken window into safe leafiness. The other purrs under my delighted brother's pats. The floor is littered, sticky, with feces. The down pillows drip urine. My mother goes quickly into the other rooms on this upper floor. The cats have been everywhere.

My mother no longer remembers what she did next. In her memory, she can only find what she thought of doing.

One choice is to tell Mrs. Perren, perhaps even to help her make arrangements for pruning, glazing, cleaning. (My mother wonders if undiluted Javex would work.)

The other choice is to say nothing, to leave her step-mother stewing in her stink. My mother worries about getting my brother's co-operation, so he will not cry excitedly to Mrs. Perren, "Kitties pee on floor!" Surely, she thinks, the coming summer heat will eventually let the old nose know. Or some other visitor will come. (She herself never went to that house again.)

My mother asks me now, "Which did I do?" But I don't remember. Nor does my brother. Neither of us can tell her what she wants to know.

I wish I could tell her, but for me as a child that story had little to do with the solitary woman waiting downstairs or the sharp resentful voice saying, "Take him away." I did not care, either, about the reeking sodden floorboards in the spare room, the precious quilt ruined, the golden double featherstitching frayed. No. What I loved was the branch to the spare room, the branch where the cats ran back and forth in the moony night and through the green leaves of the day. Perhaps if that branch were sturdy, the window-hole big enough, a child might travel thus and hide in the heart of the tree, with the furry cats purring and snoozing and stretching their lithe long selves?

For me, this cat-story was just one of many from Before Me, stories told and retold by my mother and my brother, like the one about Slippers the calico, who in her first pregnancy follows my mother from room to room, sleeps on her lap and on her bed. Her labour begins as my mother prepares for a dinnerparty; my brother strokes and soothes the cat as my mother finishes dressing, takes up her cloak. (This wonderful garment is purple velvet, cast-off church curtains. How has my agnostic mother come by this fabric? The purple is limp, the nap gone in parts, but my mother takes scrim and shapes a high dramatic collar to show off her high-piled hair.)

Slippers struggles up and follows my mother, mewing, one scarcely-born kitten left behind in the basket and another's nose sticking out of her vagina. My brother retrieves the cat, but Slippers writhes and yowls and my brother, fearful, drops her. She runs after my mother and half-way down the stairs delivers her second kitten. My mother stops. She gathers cat and kitten into her cloak. She brings them back to the basket in her bedroom. My brother has to go downstairs and tell my father, waiting impatiently in the livingroom with the fire going out, that she isn't coming. She settles down with Slippers, and the kittens are born in peace. When all are safely curled by their mother, she does go to the party, where she makes a fine story out of the event and my father almost forgives her.

And another story is of the cat Johnny-come-lately, of a winter's dusk, thick snow falling, my brother by the livingroom gazing, half-dreaming with the white movement of the flakes. A red car comes along—an uncommon colour in 1930s Toronto—and stops by our house. My brother calls, "Mum, come look at the red car." The moment she appears at the window, the car opens, a black kitten is flung out, and the car flees scarlet down the street, with rooster tails of snow and exhaust whirling behind it. Johnny, who lived with our family for years, was the first animal whose death I grieved.

My mother wants me to tell her the ending of the story about the visit so she will know whether she did right or wrong. Did she obey duty or desire? Which was which? Without the memory, she cannot judge herself.

I want other knowledge. I want to know why my mother forgot my grandfather. She has never in my presence pronounced the term *Dad*, never used the words, "I remember when my father . . . ." No snapshot or painting is extant. No letters survive, account books, diaries. No stories. But a beautiful joyous woman married him; she must have had her reasons, and I wish I knew what they were.

Did my mother feel such abandonment that when she grew up she simply obliterated him from the stones of memory? Did she unilaterally declare herself fatherless as well as motherless? Her mother was always dead, a person who existed only in stories, none told by her father. None of his words have survived. Nor has he. At this point in the story, I have said every single thing I know about him.

I'll try to imagine. Let us suppose that after my mother's birth my grandfather sits by my grandmother's bedside, looking down at her lovely face, seeing with delight his living daughter. Likely he goes away then, to tell family and friends, perhaps to thank his God for the safe deliverance this time, to sleep at night and wake joyful in the morning. But by then the dirt, the poison, is thick in her blood. She feels unwell. The doctor comes. The milk stops. The baby cries. The smells begin. *The patient is toxic and febrile, the lochia is foul-smelling, and the uterus is tender . . . .* The young woman lies quietly. *Chills, headache, malaise, and anorexia are common. Pallor, tachycardia, and leukocytosis are the rule.* This rule holds. So as she dies my grandmother does not scream and writhe and froth like the cat, but slowly dazes and drifts, descending into a poisoned stupor *(Hemolytic anemia may develop . . . .With severe hemolysis and coexistent toxicity, acute renal failure is to be expected)* and so to her death. *The* mortality rate is then about fifty percent. But then there was neither debridement nor penicillin, so that rate did not apply. The father sends the child off to live with her grandparents. What else to do? My great-grandparents love the baby, painfully. They live nearby. He cannot be a saddler and care for an infant on his own. Paid help is not possible. So for five years the little girl lives thus. Then—inexplicably, to such a young child—comes the alleged reunion, which is in truth a meeting with a cold bitter woman who resents her step-daughter even before they meet, who teaches an innocent girl to believe herself to be evil, who burns her present and makes her witness the agony of the cat.

In his third marriage, how came my grandfather to make such an error in judgment?

In my fifteenth summer, our plump tabbycat Mitzi with the extra toes dies on the operating table as she is being spayed. My mother collapses with grief, self-blame, rage at herself and my father for having determined that this cat should not kitten. "She mewed all the way in the car," my mother shouts, weeping, her sweating face contorted. "She didn't want to go. I made her. Because I was bigger and stronger. I took her to her death." My mother falls on the sofa and shoves her head into the cushions and hits the sofa arm repeatedly. My father and I look at each other. I start to leave the room. "You can't run away from this," he says, gripping my arm hard. "Come back to her."

Somehow the afternoon comes to its end. My mother does not make any dinner, and this is very difficult for me because my father likes no cooking but hers. Early in the evening, she goes up to the spare room in the attic and closes the door. She stays there overnight. We hear her crying from time to time, and shoving at the stiff window; finally it surrenders to her strength, with a harsh scraping rattle of glass against wood. In the spare room are stored non-working lamps, moth-nibbled blankets, magazines that my brother will sort through some day. The bed is not made up. Faded chenille covers its lunar surface. The heart of the house beats in the wrong place that night, and, though the spare room is next to mine, I gain no comfort from my mother's nearness. Thinking of her there disturbs me still.

The Man, the Woman, and the Witch of New Orleans

This man, George, has been married to this woman, Eileen, for eight full years and a day, and still wants often to make love with her. And he does so; she wants as much, as often. Standing at a supermarket checkout or in a movie lineup or at a buffet in a friend's house, George looks at Eileen and knows that she feels just as he does, i.e., that the faster they can get home upstairs unclothed abed the very much better everything will be.

What is the matter, then?

He is not content with their lovemaking.

This man is potent. He loves the long mutual pleasuring he experiences with his wife, wherein he feels sweetness not just in his genitals but throughout his corporeal mass. And he knows that he delights Eileen. How? Her body tells him. So do the words that come out of her sweet mouth.

What does Eileen look like? Oh beautiful—beautiful as the coast of British Columbia, the Inside Passage, temperate, fretted and filigreed with islands, green, a thousand sunlit greens all flailed and wrapped and veiled with rain and salt.

In short, George finds happiness in every part of her, all herself, and also in her happiness in him.

What then in heaven's name is his problem?

Eileen says, "George," and they pay for the groceries or leave the lineup or make their excuses. They go home to their bed. So? This man's problem is that he wants to be underneath. More precisely, he wants to *feel* underneath: controlled, ridden, dominated. He wants to abandon himself to the knowledge that someone else will decide.

Now George is well informed about the importance of open communication between partners, and has therefore expressed his desire to be underneath; he has both verbally and physically expressed it to Eileen, when lying with her, in the early or intermediate stages of lovemaking when conscious choice remains possible; and, because of the particular enjoyments that configuration affords Eileen, she is more than willing to be on top. But still what George wants does not happen. He is under but not really under. Not really.

This problem, then, is in George's head, where it occupies too much of his time, taking him down strange tracks of thought along which he deeply does not wish to go, such as wondering if at some level he may desire to be beaten, chained, cut, whipped.

This problem is a variation on the old saw about the necessary invention of God, for, in all other respects, the life of Eileen and George is a model of modest affluence, suitable tastes, and unremarkable opinion.

This problem leads George, when Eileen suggests they take a holiday elsewhere than on a Gulf Island, to agree with enthusiasm after only a short period of uncertainty, for he reasons that a puzzle hardened in Vancouver may prove soluble in novel surroundings.

They do not pick a Caribbean country or Cuba, because those dubious places are not what George and Eileen are accustomed to. George often goes to San Francisco on business, so that city is out, and they are sure that New York is too dirty. Europe is too far. One day when George comes home from work—he is a partner in a firm of management consultants—Eileen shows him the current issue of the auto association magazine. New Orleans sounds perfect. Different, but not too different; south, but still in North America. Also, George's father went there in 1948 to visit an old friend from elementary school in Chatham, Ontario, who had curiously enough ended up in the Louisiana tobacco business, and George's father had had a good time.

So George and Eileen fly to New Orleans in one of those great aluminum birds.

The city of New Orleans, built on clamshells and river sand along a crescent moon of the Mississippi and well below the level of that river, exists in pulsating tension between decay and new growth. A child's wooden wagon left out for a fortnight grows a green skin, while a vine sprouts and begins to twine about the toy. In their elevated graves, in vast glare-white cities of the dead, black and white New Orleanians rot so briskly that one modest tomb may readily hold all that's left of a hundred and seventeen nuns and yet stand ready to take on dozens more. Once, the local foods were highly spiced to delay or mask corruption. Still spiced, they are now refrigerated, frozen, microwaved, convected . . . but still the spoon sinks into the fragrant, maybe, gumbo, like a foot into the marshes by the Gulf. What lies beneath that surface? What condition is it in? Delicious . . . . Rot, mould, rust, peel, blister, burst, sag, mildew—against these ferocious verbs the citizenry send forth one noun: paint. Coat upon coat upon coat of paint, white and cream and pearl and bone and ivory and palest rose. Paint to fill, seal, protect, prevent, maintain. Barely, until next year. Throughout the city, fish and mud smell hairily in the nostrils. Sun and green contend. The full-leaved summer sky is green heat.

George and Eileen arrive at dusk. At the hotel registration desk, they do not immediately realize that the (white) receptionist is speaking English to them. Then the (black) bellhop takes them to Room 777, oh delight, a magic number, and standing in the iced rose chamber they see approvingly the little fridge, the microwave, the television, the telephone, the air-conditioner, the plateglass window. They see a sprawl of water; that must be the Mississippi, which is neither blue nor grey nor brown, somehow all three, somehow not quite . . . . Eileen opens the door to the concrete balcony. A huge great fiery steamy mouth billows into the room and practically swallows them up in two seconds flat. George closes the door. Tired from the flight and the lost luggage, their bodies suffused with an ambiguous sensation of being dreadfully hot and yet chilly, he and Eileen look at each other and say "Well." They do not make love that night.

Next morning when they go down for breakfast in the hotel coffee shop, the waitress is a witch. George can tell right away. The witchiness is on her like condensation on a mint julep cup. She stands between him and Eileen—well, naturally she would, since they are on opposite sides of a small table, but George does not think of that—and he can feel the spellbinding. Mostly it seems to come from her eyes. Invisible membranes link his frame with hers. Her skin is white against the smart black uniform, beneath which are high breasts; George knows precisely how it would feel to lie on the coffee shop floor and watch those nipples drop to his hands, his lips. The witch's lips are moving. "Apple?" Her navel is at his eye-level. His tongue will go deep in that curious little blind mouth. She is surely leaning towards him . . . .

"No, not apples this morning," says Eileen. She suggests that they try café au lait. They do. The combination of sharp chicory and soft milk delights them both. They drink two cups each, while eating just-baked brioches with French quince jam, and are truly on holiday. Refreshed, they take the St. Charles streetcar out to the Zoo, where they spend the morning exclaiming at the wild flashes of the tropical birds and the ecstatic slumbers of the hippopotami. Did Eileen notice anything?

The witch is there again right after lunch when George goes down to the lobby to buy a newspaper. (Eileen is having a New Orleans siesta, but George is against wasting time when on holiday.) Waiting for the Up elevator, wondering what *Picayune* means, George is suddenly aroused. He turns to see the witch waving through the plateglass window of the coffee shop. He darts into the mercifully arriving elevator. She smiles at him.

Those apple cheeks swell. She draws her hand across the front of her uniform. As the doors close, George's body moves involuntarily. He longs to feel her descending weight. George rides the elevator up to the twentieth floor and down to the seventh several times, chatting briefly on one trip with a man named Josh who is attending a convention of pesticide salesmen; Josh can neither find his key nor remember his room number. Discussing these problems, George gratefully feels himself subside. He finds Eileen with her eyes still closed.

The witch is not there when Eileen and George come down a little later to take their afternoon bus tour of New Orleans. In relief, George exudes an extra pint or so of sweat as they walk across the blazing hotel concourse to the airconditioned bus. When he finds that the busdriver is affable and humorous and black, George is conscious of happiness, hugs Eileen and says, "You had the right idea." He knows he will enjoy this tour. He does. They both do. They see everything, everything. The Superdome. Lake Pontchartrain (punchatrain), a bland milky blue, an indefinable horizon. They see Tulane University. The Zoo—they tell the other tourists what's best to see. The Garden District and Millionaires' Row. The Pontalba and Jackson Square. The French Quarter. The old slave market. The City Park. The Museum. A giant cemetery. The Mississippi, now a sparkling multicoloured flow . . . it is unlike, unlike home. It is what they have come for. It is wonderful. They take pictures. Even the manhole covers are exotic and they both photograph them, Eileen and George bending over like giggling flamingos on Terpsichore Street as they focus on the cast iron moon and stars. (Eileen's photo turns out so well that later in the year she and George order prints and make really quite unique Christmas cards.)

The only untoward event of the day is that George goes to sleep right after a cosy room service dinner, and when he wakes in the night and sees Eileen radiant under the moon he does not feel able to touch her, because she hates to be awakened while getting her eight hours. So they do not make love then either. Trying to repel visions of the black uniform and the flesh beneath, George lies awake for some time.

When he wakes, late next morning, Eileen has gone down to the coffee shop and bought a treat for him: a baked apple. George loves baked apples. The amber sphere, girt about with whipped cream and peaked with almonds, sits in its sundae dish like a small fat queen on her throne. One touch of the spoon, and the pierced puffed skin collapses. The fruit, a Florida apple, is extremely sweet, and George thinks with longing of a baked Northern Spy or even a B.C. Macintosh . . . but he spoons up every bit of his breakfast. George feels so good all over, so happy, that he wants to hold his wife, to feel her warmth without and within—but she is all dressed for sightseeing.

Later, during their self-guided walking tour of the Garden District, the two stop at a corner store to buy cold drinks. The black woman at the cash register, comfortable, middle-aged, says, "Hah yall honey?" and "You come on back real soon now, honey, year?" These extraordinary remarks, coupled with the cool flow of root beer and Dr. Pepper, make Eileen and George feel better. They have quarrelled. They have walked around and along too many green-shrouded blocks, past too many great houses like bricks of vanilla ice cream about to melt in the mesmerizing air. They have photographed the recurrent trio of buildings—big house, slave quarters, *garconniere*, big house, slave quarters, *garconniere*—so many times that they wonder whether or not they have already taken that one there with the green shutters and the ivy . . . . George has several times tripped over the thrusting roots of the liveoak trees, roots that heave and crack the sidewalks and expose the layered clamshells and river sand beneath.

What is the subject of their quarrel? Yesterday the busdriver told them, as they viewed a street or so of this same Garden District, that the *garconnieres* came to be because the young boys in one of the big beautiful white houses played with fire. And so, the driver said, the custom developed that when the sons of the plantation owners, whose city dwellings these elegant houses were, came to puberty, they moved out of the big buildings and into smaller ones especially designed for them, which were easier of control in case of conflagration. Smoothly, the driver then segued into the story of the cornstalk house, charming . . . . And so this morning George has simply remarked, "Good idea, packing kids off on their own like that," and Eileen has answered sharply, "George, you don't for one minute think that's the real story, do you?" Both feel adrenalin move through their veins, which do not at all welcome the additional heat.

The cool duskiness of this little store is so pleasant, the woman's voice so soothing, that George and Eileen do not walk out into the hot rubbery street again but stand inside, sipping, and looking about them at the booths along one wall, the big slow fans whirring and humming in the dim air by the ceiling. Above a counter at the back of the store a leathery old sign lists po' boys, thirty-five different kinds. They look at one another. They agree. Because that feels good they smile and then, laughing outright, they sit down. Soon they get long buttered blimps of crusty bread, piled with spiced sausage. It is not like anything back home. They wash down this good food with further tankards of cold pop and are happy again. Eileen says, "It's like being teenagers on a date," and they look at each other. Then a man emerges from the kitchen. Walking stiffly, he comes toward their booth. He takes a chair from a nearby table and sits down with them. This man is sixty perhaps, white, with a crewcut that says Army and corrugated skin that says Heavy smoker and eyes that say No new ideas in here. He wears a red boiler suit, stained, faded.

"That woman," he says, jerking with his thumb towards the cash register, "I hate her." (Actually he says *Ah hates uh*, but in the interests of clarity and emphasis no further attempt will be made to represent the accent.) "I hate her. I'd like to put my hands around her skinny nagging neck and squeeze."

By a flicker of her eyes, the black woman indicates to George and Eileen *Don't worry*, but the current grouping of bread and sausage and butter stays still in George's mouth.

"I'd squeeze," continues the man in the red boiler suit, "I'd squeeze till all the living life was out of that mean body. That woman. What that woman has done to me? Mean. Hating. Hard." (A bang with the fist on the knee accompanies each term.) "Yes, a cruel woman and a suspicious one, a bitter woman and a spiteful one." (Here the man's voice becomes sing-song and horrified George finds that he is chewing in synch.) "A woman who's taken me and wrung me, wrung me like a dish-cloth and flung me, flung me into the farthest farthest corner of the sink. Yeah." The man stands up and hitches his chair forward so he can comfortably lean his elbows on George and Eileen's table. They inch towards the wall. "Yeah. Wrung me, flung me, damn near hung me." The man slaps the flat of his hand so hard on their table top that all the bottles of hot sauce and piquant sauce and pickled peppers leap up and down.

"Enough," says the woman at the cash register. The man gets up, replaces the chair, walks out back to the kitchen area. "He don't know what he's talking about. Truly he don't," says the woman. "Not even what he's thinking about." She accepts George's money with a broad smile and walks out back. As they leave, George and Eileen glance kitchenwards. Through the doorway they can see the man in the red boiler suit sitting on a chair, his back to them. Across his shoulder lies a round black arm, and a black hand comfortably pats that shoulder. All that they can see of his right arm is extended rightward in a curving movement, a movement to enfold.

George then does not want to go back to the hotel so Eileen can have a nap. He wants to go to the Cabildo, the Jax Building, the Café du Monde, and reminds Eileen sharply of the brevity of their visit.

After the long streetcar ride, after the pushing pressing walk through the crowds of the Quarter, through the raunchy loud alleys lit with neon under the blaring sun, George is himself spent. He is hot through and through. He is not sure how he feels, not sure that he may not be getting ill. Briefly, the tempera-ture preserved by the thick stone walls of the Cabildo refreshes him; he has found that the omnipresent airconditioning of New

Orleans enervates rather than cools, and at first he takes pleasure in the dim cellary feeling of the old building. But much of it is blocked off—settling, shifting, splitting—for renovations are under way. On their reluctant way out, George and Eileen stop before a display cabinet filled with Mardi Gras costumes: strings of masks, black dresses and pink ones, froth and glitter and gauze. To imagine living flesh beneath is difficult. George thinks of New Orleans with its population doubled by the great festival, and is glad that he and Eileen are travelling out-of-season. In answer to Eileen's question, he does not like any of those dresses; when directed to look more carefully at that black one, he concedes its smartness.

Then they are out in the heat again, under the heat, through the heat, walking by the Café du Monde. Café au lait—no, thick, fatty, curdling in the stomach. Beignets—no, sticky, greasy. And so they arrive at the public market and its colours, smells, crowds, calls, white skins, dark skins, chocolates, coffees, pralines, porcelains, prices, touching, pushing, fish-eyes glazed and glaring, pricetags, tourist prices, t-shirts, pennants, plastic cups with Tara on them, Tara, Tara, Tara. Shrimps and prawns and crayfish, no, no fresh crayfish, for they are travelling out of season. Redfish. Fish. Up there, on the other side of the levee, incredibly above where George and Eileen and all this awful mass of people stand now, is the river. The river. Old Man River. The plaque on this building says it used to be the slave market. The market for slaves. The public market for slaves. People who were bought and sold, sold and bought, owned by other people. George feels dizzy, and sits down on a bench. Eileen sits down. She is pale. In front of them is a phone booth. They sit. They do not do or say anything.

George says, "I'm going to call Dad's old friend." At the phone booth, by mistake he rests his bare arm on the metal shelf. He cries out. He turns the pages. "No listing." He comes back and sits down beside Eileen; they hold hands. They look fully at the slave market. George is still upset but somewhere a long way inside part of him feels better.

"That nice woman," George says, remembering. "Why did he say he hated her?"

"He doesn't know how to see what he is," Eileen says tremulously. George forgets all about the man in his immediate concern for Eileen, and in vehement and ultimately triumphant attempts to get a taxi back to the hotel.

There, Eileen lies down on the bed and arranges the cool cotton folds about her limbs. Almost immediately she sleeps. George tries to but can't. He plays with the remote control on the TV, looks at the thriller he started on the plane, gets a few clues in the *Picayune* crossword, but mostly he waits for Eileen to wake up. When she does, she says she feels grubby, sweaty, messy, and she is going to do a Complete. George sighs. A Complete is a bath and a shower and a shampoo and a manicure and an application of many bottled substances; it is not brief.

"George," says Eileen, coming naked out of the bathroom and looking not at all at her husband but at a bottle in her hand, "could you go down to the drugstore in the lobby and buy me some more clear nail polish?"

As he emerges from the drugstore George feels panic. He is right. The witch awaits.

The lobby, the elevator, a hallway, a door pass in speedy succession through George's consciousness, and then he is in an odd little room where uniforms hang in polyester phalanxes and the air is flavoured with deodorants, mousses, gels. There is a narrow bed, perhaps an army cot. With magical swiftness, the witch peels off all her clothes and his clothes and has him lying flat on his back and slips first a condom and then herself on to him. Those nipples are in his hands, then the breasts lie soft and big on his chest, the tongue is deep in his mouth, the thighs—these are muscular—are tight along the sides of his panting body, and her body has sucked in every inch of him (George feels there may perhaps be a yard).

The witch moves with slow authoritative vigour, shunting George a little up the bed with every fall and rise. A rich smell of cinnamon emanates from her. Today is the first time in

George's life that he has seen two naked women within ten minutes. Also, overtaken though he is, undone, unable to do a thing except what the witch firmly indicates he is to do with his fingers, some memory is trying to surface in his bewildered consciousness. She is moving harder and faster now. George worries that she will slam his head against the wall, but she gives him a brisk quarter-turn, as if making puff pastry, and he relapses into his floating syrup of delight, ecstasy, abandonment, and so forth. *What is that thought?* And then the witch begins to go so hard and fast that there is not a thing left of George but the dazzle of submission and sensation.

Seconds after she has concluded, which is seconds after he has concluded, the witch leans back, laughing and perspiring. She looks down at George's rolling eyes and heaving chest. "Hoo boy," she says, "did I ever need that." Now George remembers. Back home in Vancouver there is a sign on the top of a car dealership, a sign advertising custom painting of vehicles: "Your desire created." He and Eileen have often giggled at it. He giggles now. The witch chuckles amiably and offers him a stick of Trident cinnamon gum.

Shortly thereafter, George finds himself walking with the witch down the hallway, dressed, neatened, his little drugstore bag firmly in hand. And the problem now is this: What on earth is George going to say to Eileen? For no bottle of clear or coloured nail polish takes twenty-five minutes to fetch from a drugstore two minutes away by high-speed elevator. He thinks of the man in the red boiler suit. The witch presses the Lobby button, but on the next floor down the elevator stops; Josh the pesticide salesman gets on. He still doesn't know his number or have his key . . . . Almost immediately George feels the loosening of the spell.

The witch, never to be seen again, takes Josh off at the lobby and George soars to the seventh floor, rejoicing—but then he has to go into 777.

Here is Eileen, placidly getting ready to go out for dinner; she gives him her pretty smile. "Thank you, dear. That was perfect timing—I'm just ready for it." And she takes the package.

George heads agitatedly for the shower. His body does not appear to have turned green or sprouted strange growths, yet he scrubs and scrubs. He wishes the hotel towels were less velvety, that he had a good coarse huckaback. Dressing, he stays close by the walk-in closet, though ordinarily he would walk about half-clothed, deliberately, as would Eileen, so as to touch and touch and build anticipation. Has Eileen noticed? Where is the gum packet? Is there a gum packet?

The problem is that as George and Eileen eat their delicious dinner of shrimp and blackened redfish, George in turn is eaten by terrible feelings and non-feelings. He cannot remember anything at all about the sex with the witch. He cannot remember what she looked like, if anything. He cannot remember any name, or even if she told him one which he has forgotten. The experience is a blank . . . but it has occurred, is not a blank. For the first time since he set eyes on his beautiful Eileen nine years ago, he has not only thought of and desired but also fucked another woman. ("Been fucked by, actually," says a pedantic part of George. "That is not the issue," says another.)

And now this lovely woman, his wife, his Eileen, sits across from him. Her hair and skin, her voice transmit with every breath she takes the wonder of familiarity, of the known, of the world which is travelled again and again because it is so deeply loved. George wants to travel with Eileen, to do with her what they have done a thousand times and more. As he tastes the sea-creatures he imagines the touch of her lips . . . and then he shivers, because surely, when they get into that bed in the hotel, she will be able to Tell. She will know his utter wasteful foolishness. She may be hurt, he may have hurt her—and George makes an awful face. He looks up to Eileen's loving gaze, and the dessert menu comes. Chocolate mousse, pecan pie, bread pudding, baked apple, pralined ice cream, vacherin glacé. George thinks of his baked apple that morning, the gangrenous pulpy mass, the snot-coloured mess left on the plate . . . . Eileen is talking to the friendly waiter about bread pudding.

"A regional specialty?" She smiles at George and his heart lurches about.

"Let's have it."

"When in Rome," and she smiles again.

"Eileen," says George suddenly, "what about those *garconnieres?*"

Eileen looks sadly at him. "I think they were for sex, George. So the young men and boys of the big white houses could have sex with the girls who were slaves."

The bread pudding arrives. The attentive waiter stays to see if they like it. They love it. They look at each other as they eat. "So," says George, "so. I guess the bus company doesn't want the tour guides saying that to the white tourists on the bus, eh?"

Eileen nods slowly. They look at one another in a different way, because, just for a few moments, the restaurant filled with folks from Tampa and St. Martinsville and New Jersey and Rome and Baton Rouge falls away. The slave market is there again, the trade in flesh, dark pain and sorrow. Then the waiter comes to ask about coffee? Liqueurs? And because these are two uncomplicated people who love each other in the here and now, they come quickly back to the present and say "No thank you, the bill please."

Then they walk back to their hotel, through the gentle warmth of the New Orleans night. They walk through the streets of the Quarter, now all fretted and filigreed with shadows of cast iron lace and crepe myrtle blossom. Once in their room, they do not turn on the lights. Instead, they pull the long curtains all the way back, to let in the warm grapefruit moon. Then they open the balcony door. The softness of the night, the gleam of the river move softly in. They uncover the great bed to expose about an acre of pure cotton, and on this moonlit ground they make love.

George is on top. He feels wonderful. For a moment he even understands what goes on between himself and Eileen; in the sweetness of the body that understanding dissolves, and he thinks only of the days and nights that wait for them and of all the love that can be made.

Watching

Five o'clock. Winter. Dark rain. Corinne is at her telephone, and wants a drink.

"What time tomorrow would suit *you*?" she asks, smiling. "Four? I can arrange to be home by then." She smiles at the voice of the moving company representative in the receiver—he sounds young, uncertain—and hangs up.

With her silver pencil, Corinne slices through the company's initials, ST, on her telephone pad. ST. That was the term used at school in England long ago: ST for sanitary towel. Why *towel*? Her pencil darts at the next name on the list. Ugh, so hard and scratchy and bulky. They said WC, too. Now Eleanor. Corinne dials. Euphemisms. She twitches. Allan used to call me Euphemia. Prudery. I still don't think it was that. I don't want to talk to Eleanor. Just because I wouldn't say *fuck* all the time. "Hello Eleanor dear, it's Corinne. You called me?" He wanted me to lie back and cry *Oh fuck me fuck me fuck me.* "No, not away, busy. I never seem to have the time to see my friends." Kotex is just as much a euphemism. Allan used to say I was riding the red rag. What does she *want*? Work stuff probably, whine about her caseload. "Oh, I'm sorry to hear that. Have you been taking Vitamin C?" I can leave the staff meeting early to get home for that mover. "I hope you're getting lots of rest." Good, I won't have to listen to that boring report. What I really wanted was Allan's hand, his fingers on me. Never enough. I know I told him, but he never would. "So easy to overdo, isn't it? In our line of work." I know I told him.

Sharing, listening, feedback, communication. All that time at work. Clients, colleagues. Him, never. "No, Eleanor, I'm afraid I'm not free that evening. And the conference starts the day after, remember?" Never him, again, never. "So sorry. Maybe we'll meet at one of the sessions." Corinne pencils Eleanor through and through. Boring boring boring, sitting about with women. They want me to talk about the break-up. I can feel them nosing at me, vacuum-cleaners for dirt. Well I won't.

Gordon. Now why did he phone? Choosing bloody conference workshops. Better choose his, for one—Corinne dials—skipped it last year and he was cool as a cucumber for months after.

Hands. Allan's fingers. He did that for me maybe seven times in seven years. Once I took a real cucumber. Not long ago. Oh, *answer* the bloody thing, why don't you. "Hello Gordon. So sorry for not calling earlier. Overwhelmed . . . ." Now *he'll* tell *me* all about my case. Let him. I want my sherry. Straight out of the fridge I took that cuke, an English one. The coldness— astonishing. "Yes . . . oh, you think so? Certainly, I'll suggest that to the family." Seven years I served for thee. I left it by my bed for a day, tried it again, it wasn't nearly so, well, I don't know. What's he on about now? "I'm really looking forward to yours, Gordon. No, I can't make the dinner." Can't make it, can't bear it, not any more. No-host bars, lousy food, the awful sorting out—who has wife or husband along, who's gay, who's stoned, who's drunk, who's going to screw. "Yes. I'll slip the form in the mail to you." But you don't have a beautiful bright green prick to slip to me, do you? I chilled it again, made raita, yogurt and dill, ate it all, all up. Corinne draws a neat oblong around Gordon's name and fills it in with her black felt-tip pen.

Corinne dials again. And what does Madame The Lawyer want? More money. "I'd like to speak to Ms. Holden, please," mouth stretching. On hold, always she puts me on hold. Well. Hold out for ten more days and I can move out of here. Take my brass. Glass. Rattan. Tan leather. Out. Unplug this damn answering machine. Jack it off. Aha. "Yes, quite well, thank you. And you?" As if I cared, she cared. "No, I haven't heard from him or his lawyer." He phoned about a week ago, drunk, at ten to three in the morning, but I'm not telling her that. Finish her off and I can have my sherry. "Oh. I see. When?" He made slurping noises and I hung up. "Shortly?" The papers are coming. Fair and false as a Campbell, the papers are coming, quietly through the streets to this quiet apartment to this silent me. A petition for divorce. "Thanks. Yes, a little shock, isn't it? So kind of you to let me know in advance." To give me a shock. Corinne puts XXXX through the lawyer's name on her telephone pad. She smiles. "Yes, that's true. Seeing what I see in my job, I can't feel too sorry for myself." Thanks, sister, for your support. "Yes, for all of us in the helping professions." Corinne's stretched mouth is very wide and thin. "Of course, I'll be in touch." I'll write you another cheque. You touch me, lady. She hangs up, hard.

Corinne's hands shake. She observes them. She kicks off her suede shoes and slumps forward so her arms hang down loosely and her head lolls between her knees. The tinted ash-blonde waves dance about. Slowly she comes up again. She leans back. The eyes close but are not still, for the blue-green lids shimmer. The breathing is careful, rhythmic. Under the grey velours jogging suit, the breasts rise and subside. The fabric stretches and retracts over the thighs. There is no sound except for Corinne's regular slow breaths. Water slides down the dark glass doors leading to the patio, but they are closed, so wind and rain are inaudible. The hands are still now. The nails are dusty rose, no chips or cracks, perfectly shaped. The skin is not young. The breaths are slower, deeper now. The nipples make tiny bumps in the soft fabric. The mouth has softened. The invisible eyes are still; from the slit in one aquamarine shell, a bead of fluid slides out, coasts down over the foundation and blusher. Gradually, like a brakeless car on the slightest of inclines, the lower body begins to slide. The doorbell rings.

Corinne flings up to standing, runs hands through hair to smooth and settle. The room has quite darkened, so she flicks a couple of light switches as she moves to the front door. Here she stops to assume an expression of civil pleasure. She opens.

Is it a boy or a man? Oh, very young. His dark hair needs cutting, shaping, he looks—frightened? His face is brick-red and he stands as though he might run away any minute, though not gracefully like a deer because he is big and solidly built and wears a thick heavy winter coat. Large red-knuckled hands clutch an envelope which to Corinne's experienced turquoise-lidded eye says *lawyer* all over it. A sheet of paper is clipped to the envelope. The youth advances these materials and his mouth opens and nothing comes out. Corinne does not move.

Then she reaches and her lips curve and the young man's voice arrives in a loud blurt. "I'm sorry I have to do this, it's my job, this is your—"

"I know what it is, don't worry. Please don't be upset."

"That's very kind, but I feel awful. I didn't know it would be like this, delivering things. Terrible for you. It must be terrible."

"Oh no, it's not that bad. And you don't have anything to do with it really, now do you?"

"But I do, I'm delivering it. I wouldn't blame people if they started hitting me, or something."

Corinne laughs as he wishes her to. His facial colour is not quite so ugly now. She looks him up and down. The distress is real. Sweat slides under his ears, which stick out.

"Why don't you come in for a bit," says Corinne, "tell me about it?" That heavy coat off. Sitting. Calming. Warming.

"Oh I couldn't—"

"Why not?" She takes a hanger out of the hall closet, and there is the young man following her into the living-room. There is Corinne, directing him to a comfortable chair. She puts the envelope down on the stereo. Seeing it sets him off again.

"Oh, that top paper's not for you, I have to take that back and sign it, it's the affidavit of service. God, it sounds so awful!" Corinne smiles down. "You'll have to get past this anxiety, you know, if you're thinking of being a lawyer." She has guessed right. She meets his eyes with her professional-to-professional look, adjusted to manifest trace elements of maternalism. "Sometimes," she says quietly, "you have to distance yourself. Not cold, or unfeeling," and she smiles, "but you can't get too involved."

"I can't agree with that," abrupt, almost violent. "I won't. People say that to me all the time. I'm not going to be that way." He moves about roughly in the too-small chair. "I bloody well *will* be involved. The other person. You can't ever forget the other person." Corinne shudders, without his noticing. As the young man continues talking, she goes to her bar cabinet for sherry, glasses, a tray. His voice is abrasive with intensity and response. Corinne passes by the stereo and flicks the envelope down the wall, invisible. The full glass is at the young man's lips.

"Oh, I don't know about this, I'm only here on a job—"

"Hey hey," says Corinne amusedly, "who was just saying he wouldn't make that split between himself and work? Here's to you," and she drinks her first mouthful. The liquid runs all over those parched places inside her. "You're right, of course. If the caring goes, you're no good. Hard when you've been at it a while, though. Lots of burnout in the helping professions."

"What are you?" he asks, with interest.

"Social worker." In answer to further questions she describes her job, tells stories about anonymous clients. He is wondering about her marriage, she can tell. Pretty woman in pretty apartment, plants and glass and cedar, what happened to her? She becomes aware that he wants to talk again, and so she puts a neat twist to her tale and they both laugh. She pours more sherry, full glasses, and his voice begins again. He is explaining what he will do with his life: a deep young voice, a human presence in the room. The warmth generated by the alcohol. The wind—it must be rising, for water splatters occasionally on the glass doors.

Corinne laughs, reacts, tilts the young man's monologue in new directions. He smiles, shoves up the sleeves of his sweater. She gets up to put on some music. He does not seem to notice, but for her the insinuations of the Spanish guitar counterpoint the voice, the rain. Dark outside, light inside. Noticing their lamplit exposure, Corinne now goes over to the patio doors to draw the long blond curtains. A leaf drops from the schefflera. As she bends to retrieve it, Corinne feels naked suddenly. Her back is to the boy, he is clear across the room, but his voice stops. She rises slowly, conscious of each muscle's move, and facing the curtained doors she waits for the footsteps to arrive at her.

Well. What's to say? He is pretty new to it all—not, Corinne thinks, completely new, but there cannot have been more than one or two. He can hardly manage her clothing, smooth and loose and soft though it is, because his hands shake so. On her skin, these hands are both tentative and rough; she does not discourage the latter, which appears to derive only in part from inexperience. She lets him spend a while touching her body, saying things about it in an odd harsh whisper. At the right moment, she starts to touch him. His reactions are immediate, satisfying. She observes them closely. When, after quite some time, she takes full hold of him with her hand, he does actually groan. His hands fall away from her and he lies still. An exquisite wincing lights up the young face. Watching that, she fingers him lightly and sees delight spring into his eyes as he bobs under her touch. He laughs with pleasure, and suddenly she sees him remember her; his hand moves towards her. *No.* Quickly she uses other techniques, he succumbs, his large hand drops back. There he is, flat on his back, eyes shut, oblivious of her.

She stops touching him.

Puzzled, he opens his eyes. She is well away from him on her spacious bed. Anger blasts over his face and he flings himself on and into her; she has moistened herself, so the entry is not especially painful. After all of twenty seconds he lets go like a dumptruck.

When he finally raises his head, Corinne smiles and immediately begins on him again. He is young. She can see him resisting, like clients, sensing something is wrong but, like them, unable to sustain a defence against her expertise. She uses her mouth all down his body. When he tries to lick her, she quickly takes him into her mouth. He cries out, and shortly is oblivious of her once more. Corinne remains relaxed, closed, dry. Once she releases him, to yawn. She observes how the skin of his hips and thighs quivers, how the sweat runs. The music has stopped now. She feels his flesh move about in her mouth. After a long time—she uses a light touch, to make it a long time—she stops, completely, again. Then she watches him become aware once more that he is not alone, that someone else is there, that she is there, and as he is about to reach for her, to speak to her, she resumes her work vigorously and of course he must collapse and come.

For several hours, Corinne repeats these processes, with variations. Her eye make-up is caked but intact.

Finally she rolls away and says, "Isn't it rather late?"

The young man is off the bed, scrambling to put his clothes on. Corinne goes naked into her living room. She fishes the envelope up from behind the stereo, peels off the covering sheet. When the youth reaches the front door, she is there. Giving him the affidavit of service, she reaches for his other hand and places it over her breast. The hand tightens. He looks at her with hatred and exhausted lust. He leaves.

Contemptuously, Corinne looks at herself in the hall mirror.

Four o'clock tomorrow afternoon.

My Father Took a Cake to France

My father stands before the bakery window. He is going to buy a cake for my mother.

He is a young man, twenty-six in 1928, and he is tall, bony, of angular visage. His hair is pale, his glasses extremely clean. Thirty or fifty years hence he will look, as they say, distinguished; at present the clothes affordable by the son of a Canadian Methodist minister simply cover his limbs.

In his left coat pocket is Eliot's *The Waste Land*, of which he has been mentally reciting the opening lines as he walks the noisy London streets in search of a bakery. Irony, pastry, flowers, death—my father relishes the contrasts and stirs Eliot's metaphors in his mind, sure that no other graduate of Toronto's Victoria College (motto: The truth shall make you free) thinks such thoughts.

My father is happy, desperately happy, to be in England. His brain has brought him here. The happiness soars from his faith that England is better than Canada: older, deeper, stronger, more highly patterned, more richly and complexly flavoured, more romantic—oh, infinitely more romantic. And here he is, *he* is, in London, en route to Paris from Oxford, to the City of Light from the City with her dreaming spires. Hogtown is far away.

In Paris is my mother. She is there because a married Oxford student is so far outside the norm as to be inconceivable to the university authorities. Somehow, from that fact, my parents have moved to a decision that while my father studies in England my mother will live in France. Soon my father will see her. He is desperately happy, though from his looks no one would guess either the desperation or the happiness or their entanglement within him. Dour, stiff, critical—that is his aspect. (Say the word "Toronto" and I see him walking toward me down the cold white street, his hat firm on his head, his brief-case swinging, above the snow, the long thick tweed coat swaying as he advances sternly. Because I am a girl, he will take his hat off to me.)

This aspect now faces the confections displayed within the bakery window.

My father has a tendency to stick his lower lip forward, and thus his chin; the latter is sharp and long, just like mine. His blue eyes glitter. As he ages, his eyes will not change, will always be blue like shadows in snow or ice in sunlight; although his infrequent smile smooths the chin's point and softens the steep drop from temple to jaw, the eyes do not change. They look now through the glasses through the bakery window through the glass display shelves to a woman back there in the shop. She glances away. My father's heart contracts.

He opens the shop door, and with delight he hears the little English bell tinkling, pinging—not a harsh North American buzz or ring, not a machine: a bell, attached to its string, silver trembling in the sun, the sounding centre of the fragrance that fills the shop, a warm yeasty floury doughy sugary fragrance with undertones of almond essence and ginger. My father inhales, inhales, and begins to smile. Then he sees the woman behind the counter and is silenced by a rush of shyness. His mouth goes tight, straight, thin. For she is a fair English flower. Oh, she has it all—her eyes are grey, her hair curled light, her complexion apple blossom grafted to cherry, and she is fresh-ness and cleanliness incarnate in a pink shortsleeved dress with a white bibbed apron. On her forearms and the backs of her hands is flour, which also powders her right temple just below a dip of curls.

My father takes off his hat.

"Good morning, sir," she says, and my father's heart dissolves.

In the spired city my father is the Canadian student. He is intelligent, yes, highly intelligent, a remarkably good writer, really a most distinguished mind—but still he can never be what he feels, he *knows*, he should have been. There will always have been Humberside Collegiate instead of Marlborough or Stowe, always Longbranch summers and the house on Hewitt Avenue in a modest Toronto neighbourhood (of which my grandmother said, departing thence after twenty-five years, "I never liked the West End"). There will never have been the small English manor house, sparely furnished with good, old pieces, never the youthful rambles in the tender English countryside and the boyish familiarity with spinney and copse, or possibly tor and moor . . . . Instead, my father has canoed on Lake Muskoka. The generations of quiet educated sensibility, of sureness that *This is how we have always done things*—no. The Ontario farm is too near. And on this side of the Atlantic, in Paris, Mme. Papillon, my parents' landlady, points frequently to alleged scratches on *her* furniture and says to her Canadian tenants, in tones at once depressed and threatening, "*Voyez comme il s'abîme!*" So, even as my father feasts on the Oxford libraries, exhilarates in recognition, relishes the exercise of his intellectual musculature, some part of him feels he is beaten before he starts. As he would say, will say frequently throughout his life, "All, all is ashes."

But not here. Here in the warm quiet bakery the sun is yellow in the window, he has money in his pocket, and a pretty woman stands before him to do his bidding, sir. Soon he will take the boat-train for Dover. On board the ferry, he will stand alone and ecstatic at the bow and recite "Fair stood the wind for France" and "Nobly, nobly to the northwest Cape St. Vincent died away" (both, like "Dover Beach," learned by heart at Humberside).

France: hungrily, my father will watch that legendary country rise from horizon into actual earth where he can set his flat Canadian foot. Soon he will hear French all about him. Not the crude ugly patois they speak in Quebec (all his life he will rejoice in the belief that every Quebecois who travels to France meets incomprehension and contempt), no, *real* French, France French. My father regrets very much that he cannot pronounce a rolled French R. His tongue simply will not make that sound . . . . But France will come later, Paris, the little apartment in Mme. Papillon's building, my mother. Right now he must buy his cake.

He looks again at the beautiful young woman behind the counter. His shyness begins to dissipate, subsumed by another emotion: pleasure, at the thought that this beauty will soon fade. In my father's other coat pocket is Arnold Bennett's *The Old Wives' Tale*, a wonderful novel, a masterpiece, no one writes like that any more . . . . On the train from Oxford that morning he has read and reread Bennett's introductory description of the book's genesis, is well on the way to memorizing it. Decades later, my father will recite these paragraphs repeatedly, interminably, as he will also the scene in which Sophia, sitting by Gerald Scales's frightful corpse, is brought to the door of her own death by the understanding that "Youth and vigour had come to that. Youth and vigour always came to that. Everything came to that." By preference, my father will select as audiences for these recitations people who are near either the beginning or the end of life. He will also take inordinate and lifelong pleasure, laughing helplessly, in Constance's embarrassed description of her sister's exotic pet: "It's a French dog, one of those French dogs."

Now my father looks at the youth and freshness behind the counter with an aesthetic pleasure that is distanced because for him these are obstacles that stand in the way of the status and respect he knows are his due. Further, although he readily imagines the speed with which these attributes will become their hideous opposites in the person now facing him, he does not refer that process to himself. Too many scholarly achievements, honours, points of recognition lie ahead.

Looking at the young woman in the bakery, what my father feels is nostalgia for the moment, right now while it still is the moment. He may even feel desire *for* nostalgia, that wrenching union of mournfulness and delight.

"Would you be kind enough, miss," he says, speaking formally, though aware in helpless annoyance that his accent instantly marks him as non-English, possibly in her ignorant ear even as American, which annoys him still more, "would you be kind enough to tell me the names of these cakes?"

"Of course, sir."

Her small plump hands, dusted with flour and springing with gold hair, move pointing along the upper shelf of the display case.

Ratafias, gingerbread nuts, macaroons. Snow cake, sponge cake, Savoy cake.

"I'm sure I don't know why Savoy, sir. There's orange-flower water in it."

My mother, marrying my father, carries mock-orange. Characteristically impulsive, she breaks the sprigs off a shrub they pass while walking towards their ceremony in the little London church (it will be bombed flat in the Battle of Britain). Because she loves the smell of the mock-orange she overrides my father's objections, his wish to buy her a *real* bouquet. She will plant mock-orange in the garden of every house they rent and in that of the one they finally own, when he retires.

The plump hands and the soft voice go on. Lemon cake, pound cake, seed cake. A Pavini cake.

"Eyetalian, sir. They use a rice flour."

My father is delighted at the incorrect pronunciation in the gentle voice, for he is developing a nice ability to rank British speakers of English. Her respectful attitude, also, the way she looks repeatedly up at him under her lashes to confirm that she is to continue naming the cakes—most satisfactory. Holiday cake, plum cake, almond ca—

My father holds up his hand and the young woman stops in mid-word. That gesture of his, so powerful, so characteristic, has even stopped Mme. Papillon, that stalwart bearer of the arms of the French *petit bourgeoisie*. How? When my father, having heard the *Voyez comme il s'abîme* accusation once too often, says in his solid Ontario French and with his right hand raised, *"Eh bien, nous allons. Nous partons, ma femme et moi,"* the landlady stands speechless before him.

"Is there a queen cake?" Now where has he picked up this name? I cannot imagine.

"Queen cakes here sir? Oh no sir. You must make your little queens at home, sir, and eat them fresh from the oven."

And she smiles, to soften the response. She is so sweet, so blooming, so feminine, that though there remain several unidentified cakes my father goes right off into a kind of trance. His hand is still upheld and he exudes such an atmosphere of *Do not speak to me* that the young woman remains silent, transfixed—just like Mme. Papillon, who finds her apologies and assurances blown to powder before the cold wind of my father's displeasure, and who only finds out that my parents do not intend to leave her apartment through the fact that they stay.

Which cake? Perhaps the one with the small white roses. Or that one, with what seem to be daisies, eyes of the day—some small white flower. A cake for my mother, in Paris. My father thinks of my mother. He extends his fingers before him towards the glass case and moves them back and forth in the air as if composing, or running scales on the piano.

No, resentfully, he does not play the piano, although God knows he has the hands for it, long, broad, agile, because his sister got the childhood lessons purely for being that: a sister. And what did she do with her training? What? Nothing. Nothing. Fifty years later, after my father's funeral, I learn from my aunt how she bowed, and willingly, to those terrible grinding loving pressures of family, and sacrificed—there is no other word—her own hopes (not even plans, so young were they) for travel and the study of music abroad. Abroad, abroad, that radiant word and world abroad: she diverted carefully-saved funds into the channel marked "post-graduate education of gifted elder brother." A girl.

My father moves his fingers along the air and the young woman looks at him, bewildered. What is this odd plain bespectacled commanding young man about?

My father is no longer aware of her. He feels only the intense need to find the right cake, the cake that will say what must be said, the cake that will be for my mother.

Now my mother is and always has been a handsome woman, energetic, with snapping hazel eyes and a lively play of expression and a nose as strong as her will; yet all his life my father yearns, or part of him yearns, for her to be fragile, delicate. He yearns himself to be the lover who gives gifts to this being who is other, oh very other, mysterious, unknown, in fact unknowable, as strange and distant as the inner reality of France or England is to a Canadian (this though my mother like my father is Canadian born and raised). A perfect metaphor for this prism of my father's relationship with my mother is his present status as an Oxford student. As such, he has attained an ideal separation between the life of the intellect and that of the heart and flesh, between a world of many men and a world of one woman, for he has literally to journey from one to the other across land and water, to cross national boundaries, to go through customs. And the one world knows the other not at all, not at all (although Mme. Papillon probably disapproves of my parents' living arrangements as sharply as any Oxford don). Also, my mother speaks French much more fluently than my father does.

My mother, this other being, if correctly presented according to my father's fantasy, would be adorned, no, would be veiled in lace, silks, embroidery, furs. She would wear jewels. She would recline, beautifully; my father thinks of pictures in the *Illustrated London News*, sees the languid hand trailing over the edge of the cushion-heaped chaise longue, the curled tendrils of hair clustering delicately about the slender throat . . . . As the marriage moves on through the decades to its golden jubilee, my father will develop an entire verbal routine (one of many, on various topics) about my mother, more specifically about his own failure to make her a marchioness. He will elaborate on his failure to provide her with a suitable establishment, a

suitably lovely house—in England, of course, not in ratty raw
Canada where he has been compelled to eke out his miserable
sordid existence and where she too has therefore been
immured—no, a suitably lovely Queen Anne house, with flank-
ing pavilions in perfect symmetry and formal gardens sloping
to the lake . . . . In my teens I find this routine amusing, in my
twenties embarrassing. In my thirties I despise it. Now in my
forties I feel a sour pity that slowly sweetens.

The woman in the English bakery keeps thinking that my
father is pointing, finally, to his choice, and moves up and down
accordingly behind the display case. But my father is still not
aware of her. He has dropped her into that enormous wastebasket where he keeps people whom he does not currently need.
So he moves, and she moves. Which shall it be: the one with
the long sliding curls of chocolate? with the stippling of jam?
with the corrugations born of a special pan, and these all glazed
and shining? Which? My father's hands, duplicates of mine to
the last crease and wrinkle, go up and down along the glass.

My father stops. He points to the lower shelf. The young
woman bends down. The fabric of her clothing bends too, with
a gentle cracking sound, and seems to exude yet stronger,
sweeter wafts of that marvellous baking fragrance with which
the shop is suffused. With her two pretty hands she removes
the cake that my father is pointing to, and she lays it silently
before him on the counter. The clean grained wood, white from
scrubbing, might be an altar.

He inspects his choice. This cake, of the sandwich type, is
softly round; its sides are innocent of icing; in the crack between
its layers lies a streak of golden glossy stickiness; and on its
white-iced bosom it bears three beautifully modelled *fleurs-de-lis.*

Then my father smiles. The dour face splits and everything
except the blue ice changes so forcefully that the young woman,
astonished, taken all unawares, smiles back, dimpling at her
customer in the most enchanting way. She answers his question before he even asks it.

"This, sir? It's a French cake, one of those French cakes.
Gat*to*," she finishes.

My father in turn is charmed, taken, completely, and only by continuing to smile can he signal his intention to purchase. He and the young woman, smiling, together contemplate the cake.

Then, as he gazes on the ancient armorial bearings of the kings of France, my father feels three tears rise.

The first is for the pain of exclusion. He does not want to be a king, no—in fact a long way down inside my father is a belief that no one, no one in the world is quite so good as a scholar—but he would dearly love to be a citizen of a nation ruled by kings. He wants real, resident monarchs, not people thousands of miles away across grey cold ocean who turn up in Canada every few years and wave from the rears of trains. He wants to be bound in his own person to all the glittering bloody sonorous history of Europe, where century lies on century like the multiple towers of Troy. And he wants *not* to live in a nation that is at best a blueprint only, laid thinly on hostile earth that scarcely knows the plough.

The next tear is for irony, beloved irony, for here collapsed into a cake is that same heroic, embattled, glorious tale of Europe. And is this not always the fate of human enterprise? Aspiration, promise, struggle, heartbreak—all come down to dust, an evanescent sugariness, an ache in the teeth. An aching sweetness. With that is the third tear, for here is my mother.

"What is in the middle?" my father asks, pointing to the filling.

"Jam, sir. Mirabelle."

My father sees my mother, right now, in the Paris apartment. She is wearing her favourite dress, cream with broad vertical stripes of indigo. The dropped waistline suits her. He sees her short dark shining hair and her broadlipped smile that comes quickly. Her eyebrows, strong and black, lift up and down as she talks and laughs. Her arms move vigorously—perhaps she is polishing the furniture so that it will not *s'abîme*, although this is unlikely, for all her life my mother lacks interest in housekeeping. She values literature and talk and good food and rose-gardens much more highly. Probably she is telling a story, which she does better than anyone. The gestures enliven the fabric of her dress so that the loose panels of linen move about over her large beautiful breasts. My father makes a terrible face, standing there in the English bakery. This contorted flesh startles the young woman. What is happening to her customer? What happens between my mother and father is not as his senses tell him it could be. If, if, a thousand impossible ifs—impossible as the manor house, the public school, the panelled library, the heat of summer silence on the Devon Lincoln Hampshire Sussex Cheshire hills. Mirabelle: beauty to be wondered at.

Half a century later, my father will be torn with rage at the construction of the new airport in Quebec: Mirabel. Storming, bullying, rasping, erect at the end of his long shining dinner table (polished by his own cleaning woman to the point where he can see his own face reflected in his own table), he will harangue friends and family into impotent seething submission as he spits out his hatred of the French-Canadians, the damned frogs with their hands in the till, spits it out all over the well-done roast beef he is simultaneously and perfectly carving. Then he will fall silent. He will sit down. He will cover his own meat with horseradish and eat it in large pieces, and ignore the timid resumption of conversation at his table. He will not recognize anyone else's presence, not even my mother's, so deep will he be in the caverns of his rage, his freezing resentment that the world refuses to order itself as it ought. Laying his large knife and fork parallel across his plate, he will grimace terribly. For dessert there will be my mother's trifle: his favourite.

"Have you changed your mind, sir? I'll put it back, shall I?" The pretty hands take hold of the cake plate.

"No," says my father, his voice angry and low. "No. I'll take it." He has taken my mother. He has married her. He will buy the cake, and he will ride the Dover ferry to Calais, repeatedly, for he will love her, love her above all others, all his life long. He will do his best to give her the French kings.

Meanwhile here is this shopgirl who has witnessed him in the act of emotion. He feels the cold rich anger rising.

"How much?" he asks roughly. The young woman is disconcerted. Her answering smile is not full. She names the price. Now this is calamity. Calamity, indignity, catastrophe, insult, humiliation.

For my father, buying the cake will mean that he cannot have lunch before he boards the ferry. Obviously a missed lunch is no great matter, but that *is* not the matter. A man of his gifts should not have to make a miserable paltry puny choice like this. Both a gift for his wife and a pleasant lunch for himself should be easily possible. He should not have to give a second thought to their cost. My father stands silent in the bakery, chill with rage, while the mordant juices of resentment eat into his consciousness.

Why is he poor and why are so many unworthy people rich? Stupid vulgar Canadians who could not write a shapely sentence if their lives depended on it, who know nothing of Greek mythology or the French impressionists or Dickens or Macaulay, who say *anyways* and *lay down*, who holiday in Florida (in later life he will reserve a special loathing for these), who are Jews or have funny names from Eastern Europe or both, who do not have university degrees, who wear brown suits . . . .

My father glares down at the young woman in the English bakery. He stands tall, rigid, barely containing explosive movement. His face lengthens. The prominent cheek and jaw bones elongate.

In the young woman's body, the smallest possible movement occurs: a shrinking.

My father senses it, tells the direction of her feelings, presses in immediately, concentrates his gaze so that it is chilled metal, cold and killing, and sends its force out to nip her warm flesh. He will not let her go. Concentration, intensity, strength. He makes the glare persist. Do that long enough, and the other person will collapse, he knows. I know that. My father grips the counter.

She moves, she takes two little steps back. The fatal shining appears in her eyes.

My father is glad.

Deliberately counting out the money for the cake, my father piles it on the white wood surface between himself and the young woman. As always following anger, he breathes quickly, harshly, but the rage-induced blotches on his face begin to subside.

Trails of warm water move down the young woman's cheeks as she rings the payment into the till. Then, taking a sheet of scored white cardboard, she begins to form it into a box for the cake. She works quickly, neatly, and the tears stop coming, but a damp glossy track runs down each cheek.

My father is charmed. How pretty she looks, how endearing, with those little silver designs on her face! Already the cake is in the box. The string whirls off a ball suspended from the ceiling. She manipulates it deftly so the fibre goes over and under and round and about. Quickly, there is the finished box. She has even provided a pair of carrying loops through which my father can put his fingers; hers leave the loops and so push the cake box across the counter towards him.

"That is very pretty," my father says admiringly. Surprised that the young woman does not respond, he rephrases his compliment. "You do that very well."

To this she does respond, in a manner archetypal among people interacting with my father. She smiles—a little, not fully—and utters a null monotonous answer, not meeting his eyes. "It is a butterfly knot, sir."

Then she walks through a doorway behind the counter and closes the door.

My father stands alone in the warm quiet fragrant room.

A few months before my father's death, he sits with my mother in their sunny garden, near the roses blooming by his study door, and reads aloud a letter from an old friend on holiday in France. This friend refers, amid descriptions of landscape and weather and food, to the servants at the country house where he is staying.

My father cries. Beating his thin hand on his thin knee, he asks shrilly why he has been stuck in this hole in Canada, why he has not been the one chosen for the sojourn in the well-staffed

French chateau. Why has he been exiled to the Siberia of the scholar's life in this country where no one appreciates him or his abilities? Why did there not exist, when he was young, the plethora of scholarships and fellowships for study abroad available now to every Tom Dick and Harry who manages for God's sake to scrape through a general arts B.A.? Around him flowers the radiant garden that my mother has created, loving every hour of the labour involved. The flower beds give way to plain lawn, where crab-apples stand, and this lawn in turn slopes down to a duck-spotted brook overhung with willows. Inside, in the study, the walls and drawers and shelves are thick with honours garnered from every possible Canadian source.

Soon he will have lunch. The delicious Italian chicken soup, with tortellini, is based on a stock that takes my mother a full day to prepare; in these last few months of his cancer, this is one of the few dishes he enjoys. His digestion is much disordered because, after several surgeries, his long body lacks some of its original innards, these having been substituted by a revolting and unsatisfactory American contraption made of plastic and intended to prolong his life. *Il s'abîme.*

Several times my parents' cleaning woman, a constant in their lives for fifteen years, finds my father's beautiful slippers—blue suede, a Christmas gift from my mother—stained with excrement. Surreptitiously, she sponges them clean and sets them in the sun. She tells me sharply not to let the professor know that she knows about his little accidents; my father tells me sharply not to let her know that he has seen her taking his stained slippers away. I watch him standing alone on the sunlit deck, looking down at the slippers drying there, and I can tell that there are tears in his eyes.

At twenty-six, my father stands on the sidewalk—no, the pavement—out in the cool April sun, with the bell's music fading on his ear, breeding lilacs in the dead land and tears in his eyes . . . . He has been humiliated. The day is ruined. The journey is spoiled.

But. In his left pocket is Eliot and Bennett is in his right. He is a student at the greatest university in the English-speaking world, which means the greatest. He is about to take ship to Europe where he will see my mother again, again. And he has the cake. He has it at a sacrifice, true; it has not come as he wanted it; all the context was wrong, awkward, difficult, unseemly. But the plain fact remains that he has got it. Who ever has been such, done such?

In his last illness, when he is if anything even more bad-tempered than he has habitually been since youth, he mentions this cake to me, apparently en route to another retelling of the *s'abîme* episode. He tells me that he bought a cake in London and took it all the way to Paris, to my mother, as a treat for their weekend together. He tells me. "I took a cake to France," he says to me insistently. "Wasn't that a romantic thing to do? Think of me, that young man, all his life to come." And then, contemptuously, "You've never done anything like that." He abandons the story. His face resettles into its customary bitter folds. He turns away.

And so my father took the cake to France, to Paris, to that small apartment of Mme. Papillon's where the furniture did or did not *s'abîme*. There he presented it to his wife, my mother. She . . . .

Winter Into Spring

The plum trees had grown so. Now, in full summer, Deborah could hardly see Paul as he cycled away down the alley in the early mornings. Still she waved, before turning to walk up to the house.

Slugs on the path. Phone the landlord, for bait. Paul's herb-garden shone with dew; Deborah rubbed sprigs of sage between her fingers. A handful of plums for the fruit bowl.

Into the house. Clip newspapers: abortion, oil tankers, pay equity, job safety. Put lentils to soak; the smooth little things poured and piled in olive heaps into the stainless steel. Bubbling and snapping, the water rose above the lentils like river-water over gravel. Phone reminders about the coalition meeting; hear the excuses, reasons, agreements, commitments, questions, objections, suggestions.

Towards noon, Deborah sat down to mark papers. "Who Am I?" was regularly the first assignment in her English course.

"In 1967," she read—this writer must have studied calligraphy—"my dad was a student radical at Berkeley, and he met my mum when they were both leafletting against the Vietnam war."

Don't tell me the children of the draft resisters are here now?

55

"Because the army was after my dad, they decided to get out of the U.S.A. and come to Canada. I came too, except they didn't know about me yet."

Too cute.

"Mum only found out she was pregnant when they got to Vancouver."

They are *here. And in my class.*

"They moved to a commune on Texada and we all lived there till I was seven. Then my parents split up. Since then I've lived all around Canada, with my mum. Now I'm studying art here in Vancouver, and spending time with my dad when I can—he has a really beautiful log cabin now. He built it all himself."

I bet he did.

"He's still political, too, but Mum says *Mariel, I've had it with all that.* Sometimes I think I'd like to do political art, but . . . ."

Deborah pushed her chair back from the table, got up, went to the bathroom mirror. She pressed her hands to her face, meeting the smell of sage. Her eyes felt sore. She was forty. Her braids entwined her head.

I'm tired already and there's two classes and a department meeting, and the coalition tonight.

She looked again. Middle-aged women softened like pears. Her students, then, were small hard fruit?

Twenty-four more papers. She ran the cold water, splashing brow and wrists, and stood for a minute with the towel held over her eyes.

That night at the coalition meeting, Mariel was there, very much the art student: black garb, spiked hair, dark-ringed eyes on pale skin, altogether resembling one of her own charcoal drawings.

Kollwitz must be in, again.

But the work of this girl, no, young woman—not all of it was derivative. A flavour came through. Bitter, was that it? Yet one pastel sketch showed a blur of flowers and unicorns and flowing hair.

"I didn't mean to bring that," Mariel said, putting it out of sight as Deborah explained about the brochure needed for the abortion clinic. Yes, she would do a design, bring it to the sub-committee. Yes. On Mariel's head, bent over her portfolio as she fastened it, Deborah fancied she could discern the fontanel through the staring black dye.

Late that night Deborah stirred her lentil soup while scanning the latest clinic newsletter, replete with articles carefully substantiated by polls and studies. The publication was thick, typeset, well laid out; its back cover proclaimed wonderfully heterogeneous endorsements.

Deborah added more sage. She watched the late news with Paul. During the commercials he told her about his meeting. Then she proofed an article while he readied his files for the morning.

In the night Deborah woke. She lay quietly by her husband in the darkness.

Where were the days when young women in hotpants raged in front of the courthouse, chanting Free Abortion On Demand? When dishevelled welfare mothers shoved inky leaflets into the hands of pedestrians at Georgia and Granville, flung streamers of red tape into the B.C. legislature? When the Abortion Caravan cut across Canada's mountains and prairies and pine-woods, fighting internally, holding one blistering press conference after another, making *The National* every night, its cars and vans emblazoned with SMASH THE STATE and THOUSANDS DIE EVERY YEAR—WHEN WILL THE SLAUGHTER END?

She sighed and turned over. *That was before seals.*

Friends phoned from Ottawa, laughing with excitement; every women's liberationist in the capital was running out to buy pantyhose and razors and gloves. Oh, the next day's joy of knowing they'd got into the House, they'd chanted, chained, electrified!

And before The Unborn, too. We could never use that slogan now. Mariel could be my daughter.

Next morning, Deborah was hung over: political nostalgia.

Ten days later, Mariel did not appear at the subcommittee to show her design for the clinic brochure. Deborah, phoning from mid-meeting, gazed out over sunlit False Creek—the tiny coalition office looked north to the mountains—and heard the gentle voice: "It isn't right yet." Mariel had not thought to notify anyone. "I was sure you'd have lots of other things to do," without irony.

Talking back and forth between artist and committee, Deborah arranged a special meeting and hung up abruptly. She was anxious to get on—to the doctor's for her annual checkup, the post office, the credit union, the grocery. At home were student papers to mark and background reading for a conference on the weekend. Letters, bills. She knew each deadline. Paul's workshops for the union started next week, fifteen working days round the province; he and she both knew which Tuesday was Kitimat, which Cranbrook. For years, they had lived thus.

Deborah's doctor, her old friend Gerda, was today assisted by a young medical student.

"You won't learn much from this one, Jason," said Gerda, "too healthy. Really, Deborah! Look at this chart—there's positively nothing on it."

Deborah heard her own voice. "What if I wanted to have a baby?"

"Oh god, no jokes, Deborah, not you. Every bloody woman I see over forty suddenly wants to have a baby."

"But if? What would you advise me?"

Gerda shrugged. "Well, Jason?"

The young man blushed now, although the internal examination was over.

Next morning, Paul and Deborah sat at breakfast in the sunny kitchen. Plums, fresh-picked and glistening, were circles of wine in a square grey dish.

Deborah told Paul about her question to Gerda.

The mail thumped through the door. Oxfam, Amnesty International, Civil Liberties—flicking through, they saw names familiar from this or that campaign, protest. There was a card from a friend on an agricultural project in Nicaragua.

"Typical mail!" Paul's smile started a long look between the two.

"Yes," said Deborah. She took up a plum and rolled it about in her trembling hand.

On the Nicaraguan postcard, coffee bushes flared green under a brilliant sky. Paul got up and stood still in the middle of the kitchen floor. He wiped his glasses.

"We aren't using the north bedroom," he said.

Deborah put her hand up to shield her eyes. Through the blur, she saw the grain of the wooden table. Paul's hand came down on her shoulder. She reached up to grasp the shaking fingers, hard.

Watching Paul get his bike from the shed and load his brief-case into the pannier, Deborah saw that his shoulders were thin. In his early forties, he was getting his father's look at the back of the neck: two thick cords within a narrow stem.

Deborah stood in the yard and thought of a small Paul, of not using a diaphragm after nearly two decades. Paul rode away.

Deborah and Paul, a pair of student radicals from small towns in the Midwest, had come to Canada that long ago. She wore long braids. All along their length, tendrils and wisps of would-be curl sprang out. Her broad brow and wide-set eyes made her look as serious as she was; never Debi or Deb, she wore the long skirts and gowns of the day with sobriety. Paul, simi-larly, looked neat even in fringed jeans and tie-dyed t-shirts, except that his granny glasses were always smeared from being thumbed up his nose. Constant readjustment of his vision gave him a wondering look.

Jason the medical student said, "Forty isn't young, you know, to bear a first child." Deborah did not need to be told.

She thought about Mariel's mother, coming north unwit-ting all those years ago with the child inside her.

Paul and Deborah were very young when they left the U.S., barely not teenagers. Because Paul was a draft-resister, his family disowned him, an event Deborah described at parties for years afterwards—how his mother had flung Paul's baby pictures out of the window of the master bedroom on to the front lawn, thick with snow. Her son gathered up the snap-shots and mailed them back to her from Vancouver, with a note:

"Mom, I thought you might like to have these back." Now Deborah wondered if she had focussed on this event in Paul's life in order to stop thinking about the simultaneous event in hers: attending a friend through a backstreet abortion that went septic.

The young Deborah wrote long explanatory letters to her family about these dramas and about the decision to evade the draft and go to Canada (this was her idea), letters such as she had written since her first year in college and in the women's liberation movement. No one in her family ever responded to these analyses. They all went on writing to her, though, about how Aunt Ruby's phlebitis kept her close to home and Mona looked like she'd be marrying Carl at last.

Gerda said, "Well, Deborah?"

"I just want to know if I can do it."

Deborah established the habit of chatting with Mariel after class—never before, because the girl was always late—and so picked up scatterings of her two decades: a dozen schools for Mariel, as many live-in lovers for Mum, as many dwellings for both. These talks were brief because a thin blond young man with glasses waited, reading, down the hall.

Since Deborah had not once conceived in the quarter-century since her first period, Gerda suggested tests, right off. "Just take a look at what's doing in there," and she waved vaguely at a plastic model, sour pink, of the female reproductive organs.

So Paul and Deborah looked at a map of Canada and chose the coastal city. The central demand of the anti-war demonstrations here was *End Canadian Complicity*, and organizers calculated worriedly how many marchers might be kept away by rain. Directly, the couple dedicated themselves to anti-war work.

Putting her clothes on again, Deborah surveyed her wide capable body. She thought of Mariel's parents in their island commune (*I bet he smoked the dope and she grew the garden*), and totalled up her own responsible moons of birth control. The final figure was hard to credit.

Paul and Deborah had arrived in Vancouver in the spring. This season differed qualitatively from any they had previously known; two decades later, they had still not acclimatized to the slow sweet marvel of the coast in the long months between winter and summer. On a bright morning, the Abortion Caravan left from the Courthouse Plaza in Vancouver. Deborah still remembered the quality of the light that day.

Mariel's second assignment for Deborah's English course was late. She had been working intensively on her graphic design. Warmly, feeling herself pleasurably a mentor, Deborah gave Mariel her standard talk about setting priorities.

That first fall there had come the War Measures Act. Deborah and Paul had worked with some of those arrested and knew by name many more, in the eastern cities. Demands for the restoration of civil liberties filled days already loud with *U.S. Out Now*.

Duty done, Deborah led the conversation with Mariel on, and the young woman talked—with restraint of her mother, freely of her father and his home and his friends. Of course, she called her parents by their first names.

Paul and Deborah, Deborah and Paul: this American-Canadian couple thus early shed the illusion of their kind that all political evil resides south of the border. (Or almost shed. They were, after all, exiles.)

Twenty years.

In Canada, they sank the roots formed only by people on the left, deeper perhaps than might have grown at home.

Twenty years. Almost alone among their circle of trade-union staffers and feminist academics, Paul and Deborah still rented, bicycled, took contract work as they could.

Mariel dropped Deborah's English course right after missing the third assignment, an in-class test which the course outline plainly stated could not be made up.

Paul was ready to take his turn, if necessary, when Deborah's results came through. He smiled his sweet smile as he told her so. But Deborah did not want to have the tests just yet, and could not say why, which distressed her.

"Fine, any time you like," said Gerda. "Just call me."

Trying to persuade Mariel to continue, Deborah pointed out

that dropping meant only to defer the necessity of taking the course.

"I'll be more into it after a while, I know I will," Mariel said earnestly. "I have this sense. After Christmas maybe." She often stopped by Deborah's office at the college, and agreed to design the poster for the major clinic fundraiser in the early spring. But in the New Year she did not re-register in English.

February twenty-eighth, 1988. Ecstatic, laughing, weeping, Deborah phoned Mariel—this was one of a dozen calls she made that morning, interspersed with a dozen more received—when the Supreme Court ruling on the Morgentaler case came through.

"It's important, eh? You sound really happy." Yes, Mariel would come to the impromptu party that night.

This almost spontaneous gathering was curious in its emotional tone. "Manic-depressive," Gerda diagnosed, and no one gainsaid her. Perhaps no one remembered how to celebrate a political victory? Afterwards everyone said, "We must do something else, later."

During the party, Paul saw Deborah talking to an unknown girl—no, a young woman; he could tell by his wife's stance that she was irritated, and went over. The two women held stacks of posters on which eager hands had scrawled with scarlet felt pen, "AND VICTORY PARTY!" below the printed words *benefit dance and fundraiser.*

"The design's ruined," said the young woman miserably. Deborah raised her eyebrows to Paul and moved off to distribute posters to the moody revellers.

Mariel was not interested that Paul had an aunt by that name back home in Iowa. She was unfamiliar with Wade vs. Roe, the Badgeley report, the Quebec acquittals and the Manitoba arrests.

Deborah returned, with Gerda and other women, all talking with planful exuberance. Their humour and experienced strength made Mariel seem insubstantial, ephemeral. Yet her soft voice kept on. Paul bent down to hear her.

"I guess it's all right. The poster I mean. I'm new at all this feminist stuff."

She was one of very few young people there. Another, called Jake, joined them briefly en route to a large bookcase. He was her boyfriend, Mariel said. Paul bent again.

"Do you know a good lawyer?" Mariel asked. "Mariel isn't really—my name's really Mary Ellen." Only a legal name change would do; she was adamant.

"Terrible politics," Deborah said, when he told her as they prepared for bed. She reminded him of his observation during last summer's workshop tour that the union members attending his sessions were mostly over thirty. The younger workers took little interest in safety.

The next day Deborah phoned Gerda to set up appointments for tests.

"Starting fresh, you are," the doctor said, scribbling dates and times. "No births, stillbirths, miscarriages, abortions, fibroids, D and Cs. No history of the Pill. You don't know what a record that is for someone your age."

Age: at the party Deborah had talked with others about this very matter. Politically, what did it mean?

No conception in all those years; what did it mean? Gerda asked, "Did you ever have a bad infection, Deborah? Way back maybe?"

To Deborah and Gerda and their friends—and they were all shocked at their feelings—the young feminists and leftists they knew and worked with seemed—well, frankly, they seemed tiresome. And often unreliable. And then the river of adjectives began to flow, irresponsible, insensitive, self-centred, incredibly ignorant, sectarian, superficial . . . . A great organism of discussion grew among these newly middle-aged women as they talked, in their pairs and trios and groups, as the months passed and the coastal winter opened slowly to the spring.

The attempted celebration had been a catalyst, they thought, because so many of them, like Deborah, had radicalized through the abortion issue. The ruling told them that their youth was quite gone. Yes, gone, and using these pejorative terms about their youthful sisters was awful; it was irresistible. So the middle-aged women talked and talked about their aging, about the young, about what they themselves had been like in youth and about how they were now, at forty-one and forty-seven and forty-four.

Gerda said to Deborah, "Try to remember. With an infection you could have felt very run down. No energy. Or you might have run a fever. Had some discharge. Fluish maybe."

In these discussions with her friends, political associates of two decades, Deborah cited drop-out Mariel as her example. Her promised graphic for the clinic brochure had never materialized; at the last minute, Deborah had had to scrounge a visual from an old leaflet.

And Gerda said, "Maybe the tubes can be opened. That's another test."

But. These new young ones were *not* children. They were in their late teens or solidly into their twenties, the very age when Deborah and Paul and all their companions had become activists.

Because Gerda insisted, Deborah tried to remember. She could date conferences, rallies, the writing of this article or that document. She saw vivid younger selves hearing about the Tet offensive, the mining of the harbour at Hanoi, the bullets that entered King.

Well. Deborah, Paul, Gerda, the rest of them—had they too been silly, ultraleft, excessive, given to overstatement, unable to summarize clearly the process of a meeting or the contents of a document, unwilling to contribute succinctly to a verbal discussion?

Searching memory was like studying the history of someone whose records have been lost. Kent State. The second Kennedy assassination. Amchitka: Deborah remembered standing amid thousands at Burrard and Georgia, wearing a blue rainjacket. That was right after Paul got across the border, aiming for his father's funeral, but missing his connection because of a picket line at the Denver airport. A neighbour walked as fourth pallbearer with Paul's brothers. Had Paul ever recovered from that absence? When had she been ill? She herself had never gone back to the States, because of an early arrest and fingerprinting. She had repeatedly explained this to her family.

Damage had apparently taken place within Deborah. She had known nothing of it. She had been ignorant of her condition, although to be aware of oneself as a social product was a prime responsibility of the political radical. Yes, the women conceded, after lengthy critical analyses of their beliefs and behaviour in their youth, yes. There had been lack of judgment here, in this situation . . . . They identified irresponsibility there . . . .

While for twenty years Deborah had chaired meetings and written documents and held picket signs, while her blood had looped around her frame as it should and her cells had duly replaced themselves and her nerve impulses had streaked along their rightful paths, this other inner flesh had changed.

On the whole, though, the answer was definitely *No*. They had *not* been as these new young ones were. The response typi-fied middle age; a few women, Deborah included, laughed painfully.

Mariel and Jake drifted by to visit one afternoon in the late spring, when Deborah and Paul were making jam out of the plums in the freezer. After the tasting, Jake sidled out to the living room and read. Mariel stayed in the kitchen, not offer-ing to help, talking vaguely, admiring the rich colour of the cooking fruit. Its scent brought summer into the room; cold grey light came through the rain and the windows.

Deborah now often tried to sense her tubes. Running her fingers over the curve of her belly as directed by the childbirth book under *Effleurage*, she hoped to locate these inner elements of her self.

After some time with Mariel, Paul and Deborah grasped that she wanted something. She was looking for studio space, and referred, casually but repeatedly, to the wonderful view there must be from their north room upstairs.

The women's discussions swivelled from past to future time. If Deborah and her friends were right, though middle-aged, in their assessment of youth, what did that say about the prospects for the women's movement? the left? social change here? anywhere? Scanning the radical press from Britain, Asia, Europe, the women saw nothing encouraging.

The couple did not need to exchange a glance to say No. "Why can't she ask straight out?" Deborah asked Paul exasperatedly when the visitors had left, Jake with a borrowed biography of Eleanor Marx but without Paul's opinion of it, in which he had shown no interest.

Fallopian, Deborah's mind said as she stirred the purple seething syrup, *fallopian*. She visualized her tubes in a state of health: translucent hollow stems, pliant and fluid with their own juices, like the grasses of spring. *Scar tissue* meant the wrong look of burned healed flesh. Skin it is, and yet not skin. Might her tubes shine, stiffly, like that?

The women's conversations about age then broadened to include the men in this group of political friends, and broadened again, to include a related issue. Another American–Canadian couple, Gerry and Pat, who had crossed the border around the same time as Deborah and Paul, made a confession. "None of the political stuff going on now *feels* as important as things back then." They gave examples: free trade, Palestine, daycare, the ozone layer, reproductive rights. Nothing had the passionate bite of Vietnam.

"They don't resonate," said another emigré. Regretfully, others agreed.

Deborah and her friends easily listed possible causes of the absence of resonance, but doing so generated no new feeling in them.

"Laparoscopy," Gerda said.

Several of the Canadians now took to reminiscing at length about their roles in the student movement, especially the Simon Fraser strike.

Deborah met Mariel now and then, shopping or on the bus. The young woman was reserved. She had quit college, stating that her art required her undivided attention. Mariel waved goodbye vaguely when Deborah asked, "What on earth are you living on, without your student loan?"

Finally, Deborah and her women friends concluded that if

they could take neither youth nor youth's issues seriously, this was because only what they themselves had done, as youth, held meaning for them. In this, some reluctantly saw, they exactly resembled their own tedious parents.

Laparoscopy. While the instruments were at work, Deborah lay still, resenting. Already the technicians had the answer to her query, so long in its gestation, but of course they would not tell her; she was only the principal in the case. Recently, Deborah had met Jake at a bus-stop. He did not remember her until she stated her name and specific connection with Mariel, and this although he had borne with him from her home two jars of best-quality plum jam. He sat by himself on the bus, reading (Marx), and did not mention the borrowed biography.

If Gerda was prepared to tell her the test results over the phone, that would be a good sign.

If Gerda said, "You'd better come in," that would be a bad sign. Disgusted at herself—she might as well be reading entrails, tealeaves—Deborah cried a little as she lay on the examining table.

"Almost done," said a young technician.

Another unpleasant conclusion drawn by several of Deborah and Paul's group was that they still identified as Americans. They had thought they were past that. Pat confided that she felt embarrassed, watching Reagan on TV or contemplating the possibility of Dan Quayle. "And you don't feel like that unless you have a stake in it," she finished crossly.

Paul wondered once, "Deborah, d'you think we'd have had children already, if we'd stayed in the States?"

The other women talked about their teenage children. Deborah moved her chair back somewhat from the table. She would not leave, but neither would she lean eagerly forward to hear the bitter tales.

She went from the laparoscopy to the coalition office and found Mariel in the small sunny room, sketching. Jake had a book. They were absorbed. The older woman did not complete her step over the threshhold.

Mariel gripped her sketchblock like a loved enemy and darted at it with her pencil, breathing strongly as the lines slid out of the lead. The sunlight turned her black t-shirt grey, showed the lint and cat-fur thick on the wrinkled cotton, highlighted the blue in her hair. Deborah watched the pencil move. Now Mariel was shading, repeated determined passes that generated a shaped spread of darkness on the square of thick cream paper. Deborah saw a human hand. Mariel's own moved then, to put her pencil in her mouth. The artist examined her work, held the block out before her, turned it at various angles, put it down to lean against her backpack on the floor. She took a container of chocolate pudding from the pack and ate, all the while looking at her work, tilting her head, hardly blinking. She set down the pudding. She moved her hands over the block as if sculpting with air, then tore the sheet off and crumpled it.

Mariel began to sketch again. Deborah left, late for her class.

Gerda said, "Results'll be in any day now."

The invitation to Mariel and Jake's commitment ceremony in June came before "any day." Deborah flung it down on the table by Paul's plate. Jam got on the back of the sheet.

"So much for iconoclastic youth," she said.

Paul read aloud the calligraphy describing the planned blessings, songs of joy, exchange of rings.

"I bet Jake wrote the vows," he said. (They were lengthy, and appeared on a separate computer-printed sheet.)

"Let's not go to this mess," said Deborah abruptly.

Instead they went for a weekend's camping on Long Beach, taking the laparoscopy results with them. Cold fog held all the beaches. Deborah's tubes were irreparably blocked. No egg had travelled that route in years. None ever would. She cried more than she had at the death of her mother.

Paul and Deborah encountered the newly committed couple at the airport a month later, as they waited for Deborah's sister; the siblings had not seen each other since Deborah's high school graduation.

The honeymoon trip to the Olympic Peninsula had been great. Great. Mariel giggled furtively at Jake. "Shall we tell them?"

"Sure," said Jake, scanning a magazine.

"Well, we stopped in Seattle so I could have an abortion. Then we went on the trip. I mean, we really went. We just went to Seattle too. And there was an O'Keeffe exhibit at the—"

"But why not have the abortion here, Mariel?" Deborah asked.

"Oh. Well." Mariel's body seemed uneasy. "It seemed kind of, well, inappropriate. You know? With the commitment ceremony? It didn't fit? People knowing . . . . Oh Deborah, I got a wonderful idea for a series of paintings, while we were at the beach."

"How did you feel after the abortion?"

"Oh, fine. We went to a movie."

Paul wiped his glasses.

"And was it good?" asked Deborah.

For the Record

Gregory Chisholm came from a long-established and respected New England family. Drawn into left-wing politics in the late nineteen-twenties and early thirties like so many middle-class youths, he did not, like most, prove to be in that territory on a visit. Chisholm stayed through Sacco and Vanzetti, through the organizing drives in steel and mining, through the Okies' struggle in California, through the Moscow trials, through the agonized conflicts of the American left in the period prior to Pearl Harbor.

The stickiness of the summer night slowed Hal's brain, made the finished pages of his manuscript look even fewer. Shoving them aside, he pawed through the debris on his desk—books, film canisters, scholarly journals—for the campus newspaper. He slumped into the attic windowseat and read.

"There's a Follies movie on. The late show. Want to go, Caroline?"

"What's a Follies movie? I thought you wanted to get that chapter done." Caroline frowned at the panful of black beans she was picking over. Her shirt and shorts were pink, and in the heat her cheeks were circles of plush.

Hal rolled his eyes. "The Ziegfeld Follies. Flo Ziegfeld? Broadway musicals? Twenties, thirties? Come on, Caroline. Think of the air-conditioning, smile, I'll take your picture," and he grabbed one of the cameras on the windowseat. "I don't have time. That demo today took longer than I thought it would, and I want to finish typing my paper." Caroline threw a handful of split pocked beans into the compost bucket.

A public speaker of exceptional gifts, Chisholm appeared on platforms across the nation. The short slight frame, the nasal tenor, were familiar to labour and radical and unemployed rallies from the Carolinas to Oregon, from Chicago to Brownsville. During the first of his many jail terms, his family broke with him.

"Caroline, you don't want to go just because you didn't know what the Follies were. For someone majoring in sociology, you know remarkably little about American popular culture."

Caroline set her pan of beans under the cold-water tap. "As I said, I'm finishing my paper." She turned on the tap, hard. "Unlike some people, I meet my due dates."

One of Chisholm's cousins, a Montpelier lawyer, over the years wrote a series of letters to the major newspapers of the Eastern seaboard, dissociating himself and all other Vermont Chisholms from Gregory's various stands and involvements.

"Unlike some people, I'm writing a doctoral thesis, not a bloody third-year paper. Or did you forget that?"

Caroline set the pan of beans down on the counter so hard that water slopped over the edge. "At least I take my work seriously. 'The Drive to Organize America's Drive-Ins'—even your title's a joke."

"That's only the part before the colon, and you know that perfectly well. My work's unique. Nothing like this has been done before at this level. Professor Helstrom said—"

"I know what he said." Caroline's entire face was pink now, sweating, rimmed with damp hair. Her plump arms trembled with anger.

Chisholm's family had also objected, violently, to his marriage. His wife was Canadian.

Hal found the theatre clamouring and full; the demo for Nicaragua had been successful beyond anticipation, and the collective memory of the audience generated a fizzy boisterousness, an hilarious sense of community. Someone had come close to arrest. Few seats were left.

After the Second World War, in which Chisholm served with publicly-unrecognized distinction in both the Pacific and European theatres, he came home to find that in the deepening chill of the Cold War things were changing on the left. People with backgrounds like his—always suspect to some degree—did not get jobs as organizers or staff people any more. Besides, he was almost as old as the century.

The seat that Hal eventually found was closer to the front than he liked, and on the aisle. People were still pushing in, calling to friends, balancing organic popcorn and chocolate cookies.

Near him, an old man and an old woman stopped. They looked about. Her dress brushed Hal's knees; he twitched away from the scarecrow black. A breath of unfamiliar perfume drifted by.

Then came McCarthy.

The people in the seats in front of Hal were hailed by friends
across the theatre, and left. Immediately the old couple moved
in, the man handing the woman into the row with courtly care.
His head was, for a moment, in silhouette against the screen;
it was crowned with silky white hair that stood softly
upright—a baby's fragile look above the old, thin neck. Hal
glanced at the woman's head, a braided coil of grey.

Chisholm left the country. With his Canadian wife, he settled in the Lower Mainland of British Columbia, where he was
for some years the object of harassment collegially applied by
the FBI and the RCMP. Thus rendered unemployable in Canada
as well, Chisholm lived for a time on the unenthusiastic
generosity of his wife's relatives.

The old man turned, smiling at the old woman, and Hal saw
his face: blunt short nose, blue eyes, protruding ears.

At sixty, Chisholm turned inward to resources carried with
him from his youth on the other side of the continent, where
his cabinet-maker grandfather had taught him something of
the use of tools. Within a few years of his withdrawal from public life, Chisholm was running a lively woodworking shop in
White Rock. A Chisholm table or chair added cachet to progres-
sive households. American tourists from the Western states
loved his work.

The house lights started to go down, and the old man turned
to face the screen. Those ears . . . as Porter's music flowed glittering through the theatre, and as the audience laughed for

pleasure under the sparkling pour, Hal remembered the photograph. Fourth year—a course in American labour history—with a six-week section at the end on parallel events in Canada, and a chapter titled "Social Protest: The American Way? " Chisholm stood with migrant workers in California, smiling up at the tall battered Okie in overalls. The grin, the ears, the short stature—that boyish look—here he was.

At the first Vancouver demonstration against the American presence in Vietnam, an occasion graced by nine demonstrators and twenty policemen, Chisholm took the microphone with a cheerful irony, as a spokesman for small business.

I thought he was dead. Why is he here?

Then the great tide of the anti-war movement tossed Chisholm up into precisely the sort of role he had always sought to avoid, because proceedings to revoke his landed immigrant status began. To protect him, campaigns and committees took form, petitions, letters . . . photographs were taken, posters slapped on walls and hoardings and fences all over the city . . . Chisholm . . . .

The romantic leads in the movie aligned their pretty heads and sang; their voices were sweet whines, all wrong for the effervescent wit of the music. The woman with Chisholm turned to him. The light from the screen scooped hollows in her cheek, silvered the grey coil of hair. Someone a row or two behind Hal said, "It is. It *is* old Chisholm."

When the War Measures Act was imposed, Canadian officials became far too busy handling home-grown young radicals

in Quebec and Ontario to bother about outside agitators like
the old Yank out on the Coast. The wave went out again.
Chisholm was left in peace with his dressers and stools and
benches.

Rows of smiling twirling girls in ugly clothes criss-crossed
the screen. *Why is he here?* Another whisper came from the darkness nearby: "Get his autograph, after, okay?"

Further into the 'seventies, left-wing Canadian nationalism
recalled that Gregory Chisholm was actually an American: the
great anathema. He had not even attempted to obtain Canadian citizenship. (That such an application could never con-
ceivably have been successful was not mentioned.) Worse,
Chisholm spoke lovingly of the country of his birth, regret-
ted that he could no longer make a living there, and drew dis-
paraging comparisons between the cultural level of the Pacific
Northwest and that of Boston. He thus managed to offend not
only native-born Canadians on the left but also the many
Americans who had, of late, chosen Canada as their home.

Then Hal remembered *her*. He completely lost track of the
plot on the screen. Some biography he'd read, some autobi-
ography, maybe Bolton and Wodehouse's *Bring On the Girls!*—
some book had told the story. In New York in the early thirties, radical labour spokesman Gregory Chisholm, scion of gen-
teel Vermont, had fallen in love with a chorus girl and married
her.

Abruptly, Chisholm became persona non grata in the left-
wing milieu. He appeared on no panels, platforms, letterheads.
No one spoke of him.

On the screen and in the headlines, Vietnam metamorphosed

to Kampuchea, Afghanistan, Iran, Argentina, Lebanon, Nicaragua, but Chisholm's still-boyish figure and thin smiling face were not in evidence.

The eighties arrived. If people on the left thought of Chisholm at all, they thought of him as probably dead.

A chorus girl. Maisie, Bettie, Dottie? Some idiocy like that, a farmer's daughter from some impossible place in Alberta. Somehow she'd found her way to New York and to favour in the selective eye of Flo Ziegfeld.

Across Canada, the far-left groups went into spasms, writhed, split, exploded into jagged factions.

Slept her way, probably. How else? What a mismatch. What a waste. In the darkness, whispers: "Chisholm. I thought he was dead. Who's he with?"

By now, there were rebellious eighteen-year-olds who did not know where Vietnam was (Hal found this incredible, unbearable). They thought *The Killing Fields* was kind of a neat war movie.

Chisholm's wife had never appeared in public with him. *Dragging him out to crap like this, just because she's in it.* Hal scanned the rows of dancing girls more attentively, leaned sideways in an attempt to see the old woman's profile, gave up.

On the screen, boy had met girl, lost girl, and was about to regain girl; the second love interest, based on an utterly improbable confusion of identities, had been resolved. *Rubbish. He deserved better than this.*

Now the entire company was carolling its way on to the set, which resembled a gigantic tiered wedding cake, and began a lengthy reprise of the main show tune. *I could get his picture.* Hal got up. He saw that Chisholm and the woman were holding hands.

Hal ran down the dim green street to his car, rummaged for a camera, ran back. Others, he was both annoyed and pleased to see, had had the same idea, for flashes brightened the sidewalk area in front of the theatre. A dozen older people, like Hal, were scrabbling for leaflets or programs on which an autograph might fit, and he heard scraps of explanation being given to puzzled teenagers.

How'm I going to get my shot, in this crowd?

Chisholm spoke, in his pleasing Yankee twang. "Thank you so much, friends and comrades. So much. It's good to see you, but would you let us pass now? I'm afraid we're quite tired."

People had always listened to what Greg Chisholm said. The gathering opened, a little Red Sea before its Moses, and there was Chisholm, walking right towards Hal, but she was in front of him, in her swaying black linen dress.

Hal knelt. "Please?"

Chisholm said, "There you are, dear," and in the click Hal saw the old man step back. Damn. He couldn't ask for a second shot.

She was by him then, still smiling, eyes lit, what amazing eyes, and those cheekbones, how she carried herself, look at that mouth . . . . Her voice resonated with decades of smoking. "You probably noticed me in the back row. That was my first year. The next year I was front and centre." Chisholm nodded. His hand was under her arm. They were gone.

Caroline was sprawled in front of a television sitcom, eating popcorn. The apartment smelled of hot beans and onions.

"Want some? I got my paper done. How was the movie?"

"No." Hal went into his closet darkroom.

The sitcom ran its course, another followed.

Caroline knocked. "Hal? You all right? What're you doing?"

His abstracted voice answered. "Come see." He sat on his high stool, holding a proof which he silently turned towards her. Caroline stood with her hand on his shoulder and they both looked.

The background, out of focus, was a mass of faces.

Out in front, on the left, blurred with deferential movement, was an old man in a button-down shirt, his look of love unmistakable. The dominant figure in the photograph, taller than he, younger, yet clearly on the far side of the line which divides elderly from old, was a woman who lit up the proof sheet like a river of lightning running down black sky. The radiant image proclaimed, "Here, here is beauty. This is it. There is nothing else to see but this."

The Schooling of Women

We heard that Nora Darragh, a senior on our third floor hall in the residence, was going to be a model after she got her general arts B.A. next year, 1957. Already there were pictures of her in magazines, even in American ones; for modelling, her name was Norah Darcy. We were in Honours. In the residence dining room, Nora's cheekbones angled up as she looked down at the tapioca, whipped potatoes, macaroni, canned pears. We cleaned our plates.

Our residence stood opposite a row of fraternity houses, and from the third- and fourth-year students, traditional tales passed down about flirtations, even an engagement, sparked by a glance from window to window. Our rooms faced the courtyard, thank goodness. As we came back from the snack-bar in the nearby drugstore, we checked the balconies of the frat houses. If any boys were there and if one of us had no lipstick on or wore pincurls under her headscarf, we hid her in the middle of our giggling group (eight of us, close friends after a month at college) as we crossed the street. When one of us got a date with a brainless frat boy and then began going steady with him, we did not know how we felt.

We also learned about abortions, about attempted suicides, about Marfa. Because her room was on the second floor, she was not someone we saw other than at meals. Too pale to be pretty, Marfa did not talk much, though we loudly recounted what our professors had said to us and we to them, about exogamy or imaginary numbers or the Durham Report. Once, when we complained about the food, Marfa said, "Do not expect taste, here." She was in Slavonic Studies, whatever they were. She wore handwoven skirts, beige and gold and grey, and when in her room, which faced the street, she wore a paper bag over her head. We told this to each other. We retold it, laughed till we hyperventilated.

Once, returning from the snackbar, all seven of us ran up the steps of a fraternity and looked toward Marfa's window. Then we ran giggling into the residence by the basement door, and along by the furnace, kitchens, electrical, laundry. Here it always felt strange. Sometimes we heard the maids laughing.

Nora was wonderfully thin, so she looked perfect in the photographs. Her complexion was what Jane Austen must have meant by *brilliant*, and her shining black hair welcomed any style. In the strongly-lit communal washroom, Nora applied her cosmetics and threw up a lot. She said her digestion was difficult. We watched how her lip pencil moved along her flesh to form the mouth of her desire. Lipstick colours in the 'fifties were intense. Most of Nora's smart clothes were bright, but she also wore black, during the day even: sophisticated. She went out a great deal, never with the same boy twice, said rumour, but not why.

We knew there were girls in the residence who, if dateless on Saturday night, turned off their room lights around seven-thirty. Taking pencil flashlights, these girls hid in their clothes closets, put towels along the crack at the bottom of the door and studied, till midnight at least. Then they turned on all their lights for fifteen minutes or so, before going to bed. Once, the six of us without dates were gathered in Betty's and my room (she had just finished her term paper on William the Silent and the Dutch Revolt), and we had an idea. We went round to all those girls' rooms and knocked on their doors. "Phone call for you," we called, rapping hard, "it's a guy."

Once, we heard, Marfa forgot. She walked down the hall to the bathroom, kettle in hand and bag on head. Word spread. Doors opened, then slammed with laughter. Our need to see Marfa in her bag became an itching scab on the skin of winter. "I want to see the eyeholes!" we exclaimed, semi-hysterical. Late one Saturday, four of us went down to the second floor to make cocoa in the kitchen there. Marfa walked past, wearing a bathrobe, and entered her room. We knocked. She opened to us—why?—and she was naked. Her figure was full, her skin pearly. She was like a living statue from Classical Art 110, all dignity and calm power. She wore no bag. Behind her was the window, with the blind drawn. A herbal fragrance suffused the room. "What do you want?" she asked.

In February, there occurred a cluster of dances at which full evening dress was required. Girls without dates would gather in the lobby of the residence to watch the beautiful departures. Nora was going. Her dress was jade satin, short, full-skirted. As she went out, we saw the snow falling through the lamplight. Her date's hair was blond as hers was black.

The three of us studied and played cards and set our hair in new ways. Later, we went to the snackbar for coffee and the special pastries, swollen with false cream and crusted with sugar, to which we were devoted. We had an idea. On our return, we buzzed Marfa's room with the signal for "You have a visitor," and sat down in the lobby to wait. Soon, footsteps came down the stairs. At the same time, the front door opened. Thick snow was white all over Nora's fur stole and her hair, and her vivid green shoes were soaked. She looked at us, in our pajamas and winter coats.

"You probably had a better evening than I did," she said in her high nasal voice, sitting down to take off her shoes.

Marfa was carrying her laundry basket. She looked about her.

"It's a package for you," we said, and pointed to the chair where we had put it. "What happened, Nora?"

"Oh. He took forever to ask me if I wanted another drink. Then he took forever to get it. So I left, and walked back here." The dance had been at a hotel four miles away.

"Who has done this to me?" asked Marfa, holding the package of brown paper bags and looking at us in turn.

"Didn't you have money for a taxi?"

"I said, *What girl has done this to me?*"

"Oh I never carry money," indifferently, rubbing her cold green feet.

"Why do you make mock of me? Because I want to live freely in my own room? Not shut in the dark behind the shades all the day because some stupid boys leer?"

Nora threw the bright shoes into the wastebasket, where one hung on the rim, a green question-mark. She started upstairs. Her feet were soundless and her dress hissed. Marfa threw the bags after the shoes, turned her back on us and walked downstairs to the basement. We heard her steady steps. The coins fell and the washer started up.

We were doing *Twelfth Night.* This was in our third year, in old Dr. Morgan's Shakespeare seminar.

Snow was visible through the tall rippled windows, piling on the stone sills, closing off doorways, thickly coating roads all over the university.

"Miss Beattie here; Miss Callender here; Mr. Henderson here." The pen scratched, the familiar light flowed greyly from the bulbous lamps. "Miss McKenzie. Miss McVey—"

"Mister."

"Miss McVey?"

"Mister. Mister McVey. I'm going to be James McVey now. Not Janie. Women can't get anywhere. Only men can."

She was slight, fair-haired, and nothing worth notice had come out of her mouth in two and a half years of lecture, lecture, seminar, lecture.

Dr. Morgan took off his glasses. He waved them. Silence.

Janie's blouse was white, with a peter pan collar—some of us wore the other *de rigueur* college-girl outfit of the late fifties, the wool sweater set—but now we saw, tied about her neck, a red shoelace. It hung redly down her front.

Vigorously, Dr. Morgan coughed. "Mr. Nash here; Mr. Oliver; Miss Robertson . . . ." A couple of the boys lit cigarettes. Shortly, Dr. Morgan began to speak of imagery.

But Janie continued. In every class and to each professor she issued her manifesto. If any called on her as Miss McVey, her mouth stayed shut. None called her Mister, although one professor uttered a sort of hrumph with more than one syllable in front of her surname, and him she would answer. She would not speak to any of us, her fellow-students, unless we called her James. Doing so was like speaking with cold stones in the mouth, lumps grating on the teeth and pressing the tongue. Few attempts were made.

How the boys felt about Janie, I don't know. As a group, we girls did not say one word about her, except that once, in the dark before we slept, Betty said, "Janie's acting strangely." I believe I said, "Yes," but the conversation may have been the other way round.

Janie wore no makeup. She got a brown corduroy jacket; it looked all right, but then we realized it buttoned the wrong way. She never wore skirts any more. In each class, she raised her hand. "Why aren't there any women professors here?" "Why does Milton hate women?" When we went for coffee, Janie walked with the boys in the class, and she sat with them in the lecture halls. "Why does the Dean laugh at women who want to be graduate students in English?"

Once, coming back from the library to the women's residence, one of many shrouded figures in the falling snow of dusk, I saw Janie coming out of a men's washroom, saw the little red swing of her tie. I went quickly on.

In the last class before Christmas, Dr. Morgan's lecture focused on Viola's courage and her fluent tongue. We handed in our term essays, mine on the significance of twins and Betty's on the significance of disguises.

"Why don't we study any women writers?"

Maybe Janie would change, over the Christmas holidays.

On the first day of the January term, as Dr. Morgan went round the circle returning our essays, I saw the title of Janie's:

"My True Love Sent To Me." Today she wore a man's suit, Sally Ann style, and a pink bow tie. She raised her hand at the end of class. Dr. Morgan looked wary, but she invited us all to a party on Saturday the sixth, at her home. "Dress up," she said. "Wear a costume."

I would have died rather. A long attempt to arrange a bright silk scarf casually over my Pringle sweater failed: too showy. The whole evening long, I thought my neck must look like a plucked hen's.

All of us, the whole honours English class, went to Janie's party. She had never been popular. We sensed that she came from a strange family. They lived in an apartment. We had no notion of supporting her during a rough time; we were all so hungry for what might but never did happen at parties that we would go anywhere.

Dr. Morgan incredibly attended, wearing tails and a black mask with rhinestone trim, smoking a fragrant cigar. Janie's mother, an angel with real feathers, talked to each of us in her marginally foreign accent, laughing, smiling. Early in the evening, her lively conversation with Dr. Morgan veiled the silences among us, till the punch took effect and everything got louder. Dr. Morgan's cigar smoke curled up through the ruched pink silk of the lampshades. We gobbled pastries with an unknown savoury taste.

No one at the party was identified as Janie's father. Some of the older people talked with Mrs. McVey in various languages; there were pierrots, the Little Tramp, magi, Robespierre, Isadora Duncan, Svengali. Years later I recognized Rosa Luxemburg and Emma Goldman.

What would Janie's mother call her? "Dear, put some more cashews on that little dish," and she fluttered her wings on Janie's arm. With her black velvet jacket and pants Janie wore a ruffled jabot, and ballet shoes. She had drawn on a slender curly mustache, had rouged pink plums on her cheeks. When Dr. Morgan left he bowed to her, man to man as it were.

To meet our curfew, Betty and I and the other girls had to leave before the party ended. We stood in a row to say goodbye.

I felt Janie's glance at our nyloned legs and high-leather-heeled feet, our wool skirts and dresses and our tweed coats.

We waited at the bus stop, watching the party windows on the second floor. Lights, silhouettes. Someone briefly opened the door on to the balcony and clouds of laughter floated out. No bus was in view. Chill inched over the flesh between our stockings and our underpants, iced the metal rims on our garters. We felt the lycra control panels on our girdles stiffen. The balcony door slid wider and Janie appeared, her hair bright against the dark. She climbed over the railing, hung for a moment, then let go. Like wings, a red cape floated out behind her as she lightly dropped.

From the building's main door came a masked man, carrying blankets. Deep laughter, light laughter, and then Janie disappeared round the side, he following. The bus pulled up. Dr. Morgan lectured next on *Midsummer Night's Dream.*

By our last year, Betty and I knew that reading fifty pages of prose took one hour, four hours, or nine hours, depending on whether the text was nineteenth-century English, fourteenth-century French, or twentieth-century German. We knew that writing an A essay demanded eleven hours of work for her and fifteen for me, exclusive of research time. We knew that getting back to the residence for six o'clock dinner meant leaving the student pub at quarter to, and the library at ten to. (Leaving was necessary, because parents and scholarships had paid for our meals.)

On a thick dull Saturday afternoon in early March, when the remaining snow in the city was the colour of kraft paper, Betty and I went to the Museum for a lecture on Renaissance use of chiaroscuro. Starting back, we realized that we would reach the residence about four, an hour intolerably neither here nor there.

"Let's go see Eleanor," Betty suggested. "She said to."

Eleanor, formerly across the hall from us, had committed two extraordinary acts: marrying a full year *before* graduation, instead of a week afterwards, and then continuing to work towards her own degree, even though her husband was getting his doctorate. Betty and I did not think of dropping in, and a pay telephone was blocks away, so we were thoroughly cold when we reached Eleanor and Gerry's small attic. Perhaps that is why all there is still so vivid.

Gerry's desk stood in the dormer, pooled in light, texts and papers spread out; in the kitchenette, the gingham teatowels still showed traces of their paper labels; the fresh green-and-white soapdish in the bathroom gleamed with care. All these I saw with warming eyes, saw partway into the alcove to the marriage-bed, draped in cream brocade, and to the night table where rested Eleanor's German grammar and her Racine.

Our old friend was pregnant. Neither Betty nor I had known; Eleanor's campus clothes had not changed. Here she wore a long Viyella smock, all flowery. When she handed Gerry his tea, he looked at her as I had not seen anyone of my age look. I had never seen anyone of my age pregnant. Betty shifted in her chair. No one mentioned baby. We took no refills on the tea. On leaving, we sat on the front steps of the house, smoking, exclaiming, not noticing the cold.

Was it really this same afternoon that Betty and I visited another classmate? Gilbert had moved out of the men's residence and was renting, with a friend. We wondered how he was paying. Going into the apartment felt like entering the men's residence on campus but . . . no don, no noticeboard with rules, no curfew. Ashtrays and fallen sofas comprised the furniture in the living room, where we slouched with Gilbert and Sandy and drank. Their ashtrays, heaped with butts, were the big flat tin kind that advertise beers. Betty and I added to them. I felt raffish, reckless. Betty's cheeks were rosy.

When one of us went to the bathroom, the other came too, and we forgot about peeing. From rim to bottom the bathtub and wash-basin bore thick successive rings of dirt, like geological strata in cross-section. A sticky growth covered the wall tiles. The floor, ceramic octagons once smartly white and black, was chipped and broken, and met the walls amid damp drifts of matted hair and dust and bits of kleenex. The raised toilet seat was stained, the bowl thick with brown scaling and at points clotted with excrement. We had not closed the door. Gilbert and Sandy were behind us, laughing. "Filthy, hunh?" Did Betty and I go round to the corner store for cleaning materials, or down to the janitor's room in the basement of the apartment building? I think the latter, and there encountered an old (he seemed so) snuffy man with warm rye breath who laughed when we carried off his Comet and Javex. The boys stayed with us for a while, laughing. Then, when we weren't splashing water about, we heard the hockey game.

I'm not sure how long we cleaned—long enough for our initial mock outrage (if it was mock, if it was outrage) to dissipate. Unlike the fixtures in the carpeted bathrooms of our comfortable homes or in the bright sanitary residence washrooms, these refused to shine. Then Betty and I heard the doorbell, a woman's light voice, footsteps going past us with no stop.

Evelyn, a graduate student in physics, stood in silhouette by the cold window in the livingroom. We had heard about her, though she had left the residence before we arrived. Her long hair fell straight as rain and she wore a black turtleneck over tight black pants. When she turned, expressionless though looking at us, her nipples stood out. Gilbert and Sandy saw too. Evelyn stretched, and sank on to one of the sofas. She turned away from all of us, waiting.

Out into the winter dusk, Betty and I checked our watches. If we ran hard all the way back to the residence . . . . We did run, our coats open, skidding and laughing. Then we came to the pub.

I don't remember how we decided. What I remember is sitting down with Betty at the corner table, where our class all sat after the Tuesday Victorian novel seminars, but this time only she and I were there, and the big mirrors met behind our two heads. We sat, and talked, and drank. We ate handful after handful of beer nuts. They lay warm and nubbly and sticky in our palms, bits of skin shaling off and lying on the table, discarded moth wings. The nuts were coated with sugar and salt, and the grains mixed with the skins and the chewed fragments of nut to form a mash that stuck to our teeth and made us want to drink more. The Javex smell wore off our fingertips and they stopped looking like pink prunes.

We smoked, and drank beer after beer, and we talked to each other.

I have no idea how long Betty and I spent there, talking, talking to each other, seeing our own faces in the mirrors, talking, nor do I know how many hours we spent afterwards in roaming the city streets, claiming them, moving over the snow now whitened again by the spring moon, nor do I know what time it was when we began to walk and talk excitedly across the campus, through the dark shadows of the houses and halls of the university and through the lighter shadows cast by the towering branches of the great dead-looking trees, but when we reached the residence, the lights were out and it was almost morning.

Bodies of Water

Green, scruffy, spread out with park on three sides and mountains behind, the soccer field lay vacant before Charlie, who waited. Drake's Defenders and the Bayview Block-busters would arrive soon.

Charlie supposed that the Drake, his son Graham's school, must be named for Sir Francis Drake; there wouldn't be any reason to call a school after a bird. The school's sign read simply *Drake*, hand-carved on a mossy board obscured except to the knowing by the sitkas that droop along that stretch of Marine Drive. Calling on his West Vancouver customers, his mind reviewing deadbolts and alarm fittings and electronic systems, Charlie always glanced at the sign, because of Graham—but the Drake also took him right back to the East End pub with the strippers. "This week Miss Peaches Pet," promised the turquoise neon outside, "see her to believe her." Why would anyone not believe?

Charlie liked driving through the East End, familiar since childhood, east towards home. Chinatown thinned out to the arched curving bulk of Rogers' Sugar. The Inlet shone behind railcars, containers, towering orange cranes. On his way home, Charlie sometimes dropped in at the Drake. He had a couple, watched some TV. Old Francis stood up there in oils above the bar, showing off his plumy hat, smiling far-away. Crossed swords were mounted beside the explorer; the strippers threw bits of clothing up to hang on the hilts.

Once in a while there were Drake's Nights, inauthentic swashbuckling and hear ye hear ye and a cocktail called Drake's Dram. Charlie liked the regular nights. In their breaks during the happy hour show, Sandy and Marcia, two of the regulars, often sat with Charlie. They all talked about work and kids, weather, car problems, the Canucks. The girls talked about their boyfriends. Coming out later into the grey littered parking lot, Charlie felt deeply single. Occasionally, Marcia or Sandy would come on to him, in a friendly manner. Charlie sighed and drove home.

At the Drake, a gravelled drive curled under more sitkas to bring the green panel truck (Reliance Security Systems, Home/Office/Industry) carrying Charlie and Graham up to a half-moon of lawn and a set of panelled front doors. This was always on Mondays, eight-thirty a.m. sharp, first bell at eight-thirty-five, prayers at eight-forty-five, skirts for the girls, ties for the boys. Graham jumped out, pulled up his kneesocks. Charlie slid into the departing line of BMWs and Mercedes. (The quantity of blood was startling.)

Charlie Mann's son Graham was eight. He was in Grade Three, doing fine, although Language Arts was not his forte. "That's typical for a boy," said his mother, Kay, and so, she said, were his well-developed large motor skills. Charlie thought it was great that Graham had made the junior soccer team. He also thought Graham talked fine. The custody agreement worked in well with the soccer, because Graham spent weekends with his father and the games were early on Saturdays.

Charlie came as early as he could to whatever playing field was scheduled, arriving before either team or the ref or any parents. Smoking, he sauntered about and saw the mist rise from the green. He watched the roving cats, the swooping hunt of the herring gulls, the dew evaporating on the bushes. Several of the Vancouver fields offered spectacular prospects of the

North Shore. Sometimes the mountains were only a gigantic density, a pressure the eye sensed behind the grey *pointilliste* veils. On other days they were sharp and thin, like metal cut with tinsnips.

This northern vista always pleased Charlie. Over there was the house where Graham lived, Monday through Friday, with Kay and Ken. Charlie knew the road there well. He knew it from the long dip down McGill by the race track and New Brighton Park to the soaring bridge, to the loading docks gritty with grain dust on the farther shore, to the off-ramp that spun him east then west, to the steep pull of Keith Road and the treed streets going up the hillside beyond: residences. However, Charlie no longer drove by that house night after night to stare at the bedroom windows. He was past that stage.

Cars gradually clotted the rim of the soccer field. Invariably on the other side from where Charlie stood appeared Kay's car; Yellow Jellybean, Graham called it. Charlie could not always pick Kay out of the distant people, but Graham's red hair was immediate. At half-time, the boy ran across the field to his father, carrying his quartered orange in one hand and his grabbed backpack in the other. Charlie slung the nylon contraption over his shoulder, liking its weight, the bulk of the jeans and shirt and school uniform and books packed neatly inside, by Kay. Sometimes, in the second half, Charlie watched the yellow car moving away along the edge of the playing field. The black and white sphere of the soccer ball spun alongside. (The blood's colour also surprised—such a bright red.) At game's end, Graham came running to Charlie again, and they were off together into their weekend.

Graham was a good-looking child. Charlie thought he knew this himself, but he was also told so by other soccer parents, by shoppers when he and his son went to the 7-11 for milk or a video, and by the guys at Reliance when he and Graham went with a bunch of them to the hockey game. Looking at his son, Charlie thought, "Well, looks, they're not all that matters." Then, "I guess that's about all Kay and me had going for us," and then, "It could make things easier for him, that's for sure."

Kay had said simply, "Gorgeous, isn't he?" So was she. At least Charlie supposed she still was, though he no longer saw her up close. There was no longer any need for him to look down at her short trim frame, her curly blonde crown. Only her brisk telephone voice came near him sometimes, making arrangements about Graham.

After his son had made the soccer team, Charlie laughed as he watched the practice sessions. He had a bit of a time explaining that to Graham, but how could he not laugh? The girls and boys all clustered around the ball, clung there as a solid group, so that spectators only occasionally glimpsed a rolling patch of black and white. The ball was a beetle amid bunched stalks of moving legs.

"Open it *out!*" roared the coach, and explained the game again.

Charlie and the other parents watched, with interest or love or impatience or anger, as the design of the game declared itself through the diminishing confusion of the children's moves. The players learned to pass, to block, to turn. They learned to plan. They understood. They played. The clusters dispersed. Forming and reforming, players moved like fish in an invisible tide, streaming over the green, while waves of cheering matched their flow. Now the ball was free to accept the kick in full. Whizzing, it spun, zig-zagged, flew low, jumped hard, stopped, swerved, slid in a slow unexpected trickle just there, inside the goal. Exultation, shouts, tears.

Charlie himself wasn't hard to look at. Kay had made him say so, in the happy early days. "Say it, Charlie! You know it's true. 'I'm a good-looking man.' Say it!" He mumbled it out and then kissed her, kissed her. Now, in the homes where Charlie installed complex alarm systems to guard silver and cats and electronic playthings, women often communicated their desire to take Charlie Mann off to the master bedroom right now, to suck and lick and fuck with strangers' intensity. Sometimes, even as Charlie stood on the doorstep and saw the woman looking at the company badge on his bomber jacket, he knew the invitation would be offered. And Kay had even

wanted to marry him, even before he got this steady job. She
asked him. He said *Yes*. Now, Charlie just shook his head.

On the soccer field, the parents watched intensely. Some
cheered, rushed, exhorted, yelled at the ref, screamed word-
lessly. By game's end, these red-faced adults had sore throats.
Their small players slumped silently in the passenger seats of
departing cars. Charlie, on his own as much as possible, jogged
up and down the field to keep Graham in view. Sometimes he
saw Kay pacing in parallel. (The blood looked so fresh and
bright, running.) Sometimes another parent, almost always a
mother, started a conversation; Charlie liked these chats, but
never began them.

One of the Blockbusters was a lively dark-haired girl, chunky
as Graham was wiry. Her eyes were like blackberries. Her
father, alone, brought her to the games. Though he called out,
occasionally and precisely—"To the wing, Angela! Jolly
good!"—and ran, this parent, like Charlie, did so by himself.
He wore a formal camel-hair coat. His expression reminded
Charlie of something; all season, when he looked at that big
pale man, Charlie had felt something trying to find a door in
his head.

Charlie was dark and Kay was fair, and so they had this red-
haired son. Kay had researched the genetics of it, told Charlie—
he'd forgotten now. But by then things were no good. Things
were bad, though they both loved the baby, felt their love for
him throughout the apartment, even when they were silent in
anger or shouting in it. Mostly Kay shouted. Charlie was better at silences. He got the job with Reliance when Graham was
six months old. The marriage had always bewildered him. Kay
was from money. How could it work? He had been amazed
when she showed up at City Hall where he waited with his
grandmother's gold band. *Darling* sloped faintly on its inner
surface. Kay *wore* it. Mrs. Mann, she was, for several years. As
the baby slept nearby, Kay and Charlie made love. Loving Graham made sex sweeter, for sex had made him—even as other
things grew worse.

Kay and Charlie were both noisy in bed, criers and moaners.

From their apartment in the rickety West End building ("It's perfect," Kay said, "half-way between where I come from and where you come from"), they could hear their neighbours beside and below whenever they coughed, slammed, flushed. Months passed before Charlie realized that their love must be audible two floors down. For a while, attempts to be quiet became a comic enhancement of sex. Once, when Graham was still a baby, Kay's cry in orgasm was followed in a second by Graham's startled waking cry—followed in turn by laughter, by the milky comfort of the breast, by sex again for Kay and Charlie when the baby slept once more. The couple separated when Graham was three, divorced as soon after as possible. Kay's remarriage was immediate. Charlie had not known a woman since.

"Gray darling." Charlie overheard Kay's voice to Graham, in the background of a recent phone call. "Gray darling, I want you to . . . ." Why did *Gray darling* make him think of Angela's father, the big pale man? The memory, if that's what it was, didn't feel good. The Defenders met the Blockbusters only once a month or so, so opportunities to look at the man were few.

The Saturday following that phone call, he and Graham had had hamburger-and-fries lunches, gone to the movies, walked in Stanley Park to see if the duck babies were out swimming yet, ordered in pizza (double cheese and extra sauce), and spent the evening watching TV and playing *Risk*. A standard Saturday. Graham had not done well at the game, pouted at bedtime. Charlie turned the conversation to the Defenders' win, and Graham cheered up, but later he called out to his father, drowsily, from the darkened sleeping alcove off Charlie's livingroom. Alarmed, Charlie saw the glitter of tears on the boy's cheeks.

"Dad, I don't want to be Gray Mann, a gray man. Tell Mummy."

Two words. So easy.

"Talk about it in the morning, Graham cracker." The nickname was as old as the child, who smiled and closed his eyes. Charlie hugged his son, already softening into sleep. (Most of

the blood flowed from the left nostril. The bridge was distorted.)
Gray. Charlie could see how Kay would like it. Her new husband was Ken, Ken-doll. Kay and Ken. Kay and Gray and Ken. Yes, he could see it, sadly. He couldn't yet reach the link with Angela's father, but the feeling came through now: sadness, water. A sad beach. As a kid, he'd gone with his folks to Saltspring Island. Now, a week later, Charlie still hadn't got up the nerve to talk to Kay about the nickname she wanted for the child that the child didn't want.

Every Saturday and Sunday night, Charlie sat by Graham and watched him sleep. He thought about not very much, for a long time, while the TV crackled behind him and the digital clock twitched. This pleasure had been born unexpectedly in Charlie shortly after Graham's own birth, when the new father spent hours by the cradle, his large hand flat along the baby's back. "Like fishing, except you're not there to catch anything," he tried to explain to Kay.

"He doesn't need you to do that, Charlie." But Charlie needed to. Kay didn't get it, either, when he tried to explain to her that he could not steal expensive window locks and a front door lock from Reliance, his new employer, to make her feel safer in the break-in-prone West End.

"I can't do it, Kay," Charlie said repeatedly, and then, "They could still break in, anyway." He also said, "We can't afford it." Finally he said, "I can't afford it."

Charlie still loved to look at the sleeping Graham, at the perfect outflung arm, the jaw's soft skin, the feathered trim of the eyelids. Sometimes he could count the pulse in the boy's throat. Later, stretched in his sleeping bag on the floor, Charlie knew that his child slept, safely, only a few feet away. The child lay in the same patch of the world's darkness, safe, safe as no lock or key could make him. This knowledge made Charlie feel as if good food were pouring into the hungriest part of himself. Only making love with Kay had brought satisfaction near this. Charlie never touched himself on the weekends, though on week nights he was a regular.

Today spring rains had softened the field, so the white line

gave easily beneath Charlie's heel. The kids would be coated
with mud by game's end. (The blood on the cheek was mixed
and smeared with brown.) Not a warm day, either—a chill
bright March. Poolings of water shone on the field, silver blend-
ing with the green. The door in Charlie's mind opened.
The roof of the beach shack on Saltspring Island had a false
front. Behind this lay teenage Charlie, peering between the
cracks of the dark brown salty boards as the English couple
sauntered towards the beach, she in her fur coat, her blonde
hair pinned up, he with the cigar. Through the salt air, the smoke
went up like a thrown ribbon, flat and curling. The photographers kept pace. *Who are they?* Who were they, Charlie
wondered now. Movie stars? Just bloody rich? Behind them,
not with them, walked the *baby boy*, thought teenage Charlie,
but now he guessed four, or five. The child wore those English
short pants, in tweed, and brown lace-up shoes, and a brown
tweed jacket. A striped tie. *Dwarf suit.* He walked along, alone,
looking after his parents, who did not turn, and the child did
not lower his head, though spouting oysterholes and blue mus-
sels and feathers and stones and crabs' legs and deer bones were
all about him on the sand.

Then an older woman appeared, stepping quickly past the
photographers towards the little boy, calling him—Charlie
could not hear the name—till he turned, and the cameras bit
and the child's lips began to do what was wanted: curl, smile.
Then and now, Charlie winced. "No no!" cried the woman,
shooing the newsmen off, "no, it's just us." She stroked his
hair. *Who's she?* Nanny, Charlie supposed now, governess,
daddy's secretary.

Then the boy broke from her and walked on, alone, past
Charlie's hideaway and the invisible line past which the dune
grasses grew no longer. He went on to the open beach. He went
on and on. The couple did not turn. The outgoing tide had
filmed the mile of sand with shining; the long slope lay brilliant, a fluent mirror, heaped and streaming with seawrack. Over
the waterscape moved the tall adults, doubled below, and far
behind them came the short enduring figure of their son. A long

way out, islets of broken rock protruded. *Poor fucking little bastard.* Charlie thought so still, thought he would die if ever he saw such a look on Graham's face.

Now the Yellow Jellybean shone in the distance. Charlie saw Graham's hair. Kay's car drove away, followed by Ken's gray Volvo. Charlie frowned.

Shortly before the final break-up, Charlie had done what he had said he could not do. He stole locks. He hid the heavy stolen boxes in the bedroom closet. He did not tell Kay they were there. Lying awake in the early mornings of their last days under the same roof, Charlie knew the cardboard cubes and their metal innards were useless. After Kay left, after Kay left with Graham, after his wife and child had left, Charlie took the locks right back to Reliance.

That kid should come back up the beach, stop going after them, they don't care. Come back up and play.

Here now was Angela's father, pale, solemn, solid like his daughter, parking the BMW near the Reliance truck, nodding embarrassed recognition at Charlie. Here was Angela, scrabbling through her backpack, turfing out pajamas and schoolbooks and jeans on to the gravel. Shortly, her Dracula t-shirt disappeared beneath a sweater, and that beneath the Blockbusters' red and blue stripes. She whirled round to present her finished self, and smiled merrily at Charlie.

"It's cold!" she called.

All Angela's sleeves and seams and necklines needed a good parental pull to straighten them out; Charlie knew exactly how the fabrics would feel under his fingers. The big man just stood looking, and might as well have carried a placard saying *I Love Her.* Rumpled and waving, Angela ran off. How this lively creature would have cheered that abandoned boy when he came back up the beach, would have held hands and run with him in the salty wind, shown him the spouting and the bones and the stabbing oyster-catchers, taught him to feel the anemones, to race the little bustling crabs and whip the kelp about like a torero . . . .

The whistle blew. Charlie looked towards the Defenders. Graham waved. The ball began to move.

At half-time the score was tied at three. Parents were already hoarse. The sun gave off real heat now, and Charlie tucked his jacket under his arm and smiled at the big man, for Angela had got a goal. (Charlie was grateful for the judgement of the Defenders' coach, that Graham was not goalie material.)

"Mummy's gone with Ken to get stuff for a party tonight," snapped the boy as he came off the field, sour-faced. He dumped his bag at Charlie's feet and turned his back on his father.

Charlie fingered the straps of the backpack while he thought of what to say.

"Well, she can't be at every game, you know, Graham cr . . . ."

His son's shoulders hunched up. Angela and her father were walking towards them.

"Why not? You are," shouted Graham. "I hate that dumb nickname." He ran ten paces away and stood sucking his orange quarters. Charlie dropped the backpack.

"What's wrong with him?" asked Angela, her voice thick with fruit. She had none of her father's English accent.

"Angela," warned the big man.

"S'all right," Charlie said. "Bit upset." Here it was, the dulling pain that came whenever Graham showed his wounds. In his chest first, and then throughout his frame, there was a heavy weighted sinking, a heaviness like thick congestion, like molten metal congealing. Once again, Charlie tried to think what he and Kay could have done other than divorce, but his mind had struggled with this so many many many times that it practically cried at the prospect of another attempt.

"He plays very well," Angela's father said loudly.

Graham came back. Charlie looked down at his short trim frame, his red curly crown.

"John Murdoch," said the big man. They all shook hands and laughed. Murdoch seemed unfamiliar with laughing. Charlie remembered that when he had first laughed after the separation, all the muscles had felt strange.

"Too hot now," Angela said, giggling.

Her father helped her to strip off her team shirt and the sweater underneath and to put the team shirt on again.

"We have the same t-shirt!" Graham pulled up his green and black stripes to reveal Dracula.

"Your mother gave you yours, didn't she, Angela?" said Murdoch fondly.

Angela poked her father in the stomach. "Why do you always call her *your mother*? Say *Judy*. That's her *name*."

"He does it too," said Graham eagerly, pointing at Charlie, "he calls her *your mummy*, but her name's Kay."

The whistle blew.

"My mum does it too. Does yours?" asked Angela, as the two children walked away.

"Yeah, all the time," said Graham. "Why do they? It's so dumb."

They ran, while the whistle blew again and the gulls screamed. The children's shapes, obscured by their baggy shirts and shorts, were emphatically female and male. Over their heads the herring gulls flew, random, concentrating. Why did you never see baby gulls? Graham had asked this. Charlie had no idea. Graham had also asked if what his teacher had said was true—that people's bodies were ninety-five percent water. Charlie didn't know that, either; the figure sounded high, to him.

The ball was rolling fast and red-headed Graham was running hard. Another Defender got in place to receive his pass. Graham's leg flexed and straightened. Charlie heard the *thuck* of connection, watched the ball rush level through the air, saw Angela move out. Slipping on the wet grass, she took the fast ball full on her nose and cried out once.

The quantity of blood startled. Its colour also surprised. Such a bright red! Running, it looked so fresh. Most flowed from the left nostril. The bridge was misshapen. On the cheeks, the blood was brown-smeared. The muddy ball had left a pattern, like a woodblock print, on Angela's forehead.

Graham and Charlie Mann, Angela and John Murdoch seemed alone in the middle of the empty wash of green.

Murdoch lay on the muddy ground. Angela rested her bloody head on his left arm, while with a big checkered handkerchief held in his right hand he wiped her face. Graham knelt by Angela and cried, "Angela, I'm sorry, are you all right?" Over and over, over and over. Angela snuffled bubbly blood. The tears jumped out of her eyes as if powered by springs, bounced off her cheeks into the wet green grass.

Charlie knelt helpless by Graham, his hand tight on the boy's shoulder.

"You didn't mean to, Grady," Angela said wetly. "S'okay." With a sighing shudder, she took the handkerchief from her father, wiped, looked at the mess. "Yuck."

"Press that to your nose, Angela. Press." The big man's voice shook. He was paler than pale.

Graham shook off his father's hand, pulled the Reliance bomber jacket out from under Charlie's arm and put it awkwardly over Angela's upper body. Charlie leaned back. John Murdoch looked at him. Strings of pain ran between the two men.

Angela put her fingers to the bridge of her nose. A little gristly crunch. Graham's face went clammy white. "Hell," and Charlie shoved his son's head roughly down, held it. "You're fainting. Okay in a minute, get your blood back." John Murdoch's hand passed over the red curls, back to the black ones on his arm.

Charlie's mind showed him the face of the remembered boy on the beach. He thought, *I must turn back.* How long was it since he had lain with his head on a woman's arm?

People stood round them now.

"Deviated septum, likely," said the Blockbusters' coach. "Don't worry, sir, she won't scar."

"Wasn't I just saying that mixed games aren't really suitable for this age?"

"Can Angela play the rest of the game?"

Graham straightened up, looking less like flour paste.

"Wow! Lookit the blood!"

John Murdoch picked up his child and rose.

"None of this is to the point," he said. "Angela will return to the team as soon as possible."

Charlie wanted to hold and be held. He wanted to hear the joyous cry of another, not just his solitary muffled sound.

"See you at practice, everyone," said Angela, and took the handkerchief away from her face so her team-mates could see. Her nose bled freely. Then she pressed close to her father, who held her tight. Charlie picked Graham up.

"See you to the car, John," he said, and to the ref, "Graham'll be back in a minute."

By the time the fathers and the safely carried children reached the field's edge, the ball was in play again, looping and rolling in its black and white, while running feet scarred the green and mashed it up into mud. John Murdoch's handkerchief was scarlet. Kay always put tissues in Graham's pack, so Charlie got a big folded wad for Angela, now enthroned on the front passenger seat with cushion, car blanket, and seat belt.

John shook Graham's hand. "We all do things that end up hurting other people," he said. "You're a good boy."

" 'Bye, Grady. See you."

" 'Bye, Angela. See you at practice."

The girl and her father drove off.

That night, after pizza, Charlie said to Graham, "Phone Kay. Tell her."

"Okay Dad." And to his mother the boy said, "Grady," after the great kick and Angela and blood and deviated septum and almost fainting and his goal after returning to the game (though the Defenders lost). "Grady. That's what I'm going to be, Mum. Not Graham cracker any more. Not Gray."

Charlie heard the solidity of the child's tone. Behind it, he knew the mother's silence—her surprise—her wondering—*Where does this come from?* Because he had known Kay's flesh, he knew how she would answer, in due time: "Well hello, Grady." She would mean it too, abide by it, even though she would also think it was too Irish, think maybe when Graham grew a little older a further abbreviation might be possible . . . .

Charlie thought of telling Sandy and Marcia about Grady, of telling the guys at Reliance. He smiled and yawned.

As soon as his son lay still in the sleeping-bag on the floor,

Charlie slid into his own bed. Drifting, he thought of driving through Vancouver's East End, all the way through to the Second Narrows bridge, which killed eighteen men in its making and throws itself so gracefully on to the further shore. Charlie thought of the northern abutment of the bridge, where roads incline east and west and north. Here the traveller could choose, could even choose to describe a loop and turn back again.

The Miner's Messenger

After I had received my Master of Arts degree in English literature from the University of California (Berkeley), I naturally got a job as a Junior Secretary and Replacement Switchboard Receptionist.

My first employers published trade magazines: *Western Drycleaner, Pacific Fish, The Miner's Messenger, Fertilizing California Today*.

They had fifth-floor offices on a dour dark brick street off Market, right in downtown San Francisco.

The editors' windows offered views of the Bay, Alcatraz, various bridges, and in the distance soft brown hills.

Perhaps the brothers who owned the company had views too, but I never attained their sixth-floor sanctum, and since they never came down to chat with the folks on the fifth there was no opportunity to enquire.

Operating a PBX was like nothing I had ever done before.

At my typing table were many nifty American gadgets and thingamajigs: paper with carbon sheets lightly attached across the top, special erasers for top copy and carbons, a magnetized paper clip holder, labels which peeled split perforated ingeniously. The typewriter was the newest I had ever seen, and the Dictaphone headpiece felt furrily warm in my ears.

Almost at once I was a very good Dictaphone typist. I typed dozens of letters in a day. By five, my wrists ached sharply and my eyes did not want to look at print any more.

The women with whom I worked and the men for whom I worked made gentle welcoming fun of my Canadian accent. They got me to entertain them by repeating "The mouse went out and about the house," and asked for stories about the challenges of living in permanent snowscape (I came from Toronto).

Along with all the other women, I worked in a big pen bordered by chest-high wallboard partitions. This was called the Pit.

Chatting and joking or irritable and anxious, the men— Editing, Circulation, Production, Sales, Accounting, Distribution—dropped Dictatapes and sales reports and drafts and mss and expense account forms directly on to our desks. We did the work and knocked on their office doors and laid it in their in-baskets and silently withdrew.

The office manager, Miss Brewbury, came in to the Pit a lot, to check. She looked like a mushroom on two stems and squeaked as she walked, for she wore a long-leg girdle.

One day she brought in a new secretary, a friend of hers, and established this woman at the desk next to mine.

Mrs. Kavanagh, who was middle-aged, recently widowed, and evidently unaccustomed to work involving words and paper, sought my assistance continually. On one particular afternoon, I helped her until I feared that I would not finish my own assignments, and, having shown her for the fortieth time how to perform a particular task, withdrew into Dictatyping isolation. Mrs. Kavanagh rose and left the Pit.

Shortly I heard the squeaking, and next I found myself in Miss Brewbury's office (it overlooked the street). Here, that lady reamed me out for my impertinent, inconsiderate, offensive behaviour.

I opened my mouth. Like a traffic policeman, Miss Brewbury raised her mottled arm; she wiggled her long-nailed digits at me. Mrs. Kavanagh's red eyes oozed with vengeful sorrow.

Several of the other secretaries comforted me. "She runs the place," they said, "except for them, of course."

Early in 1963, about six months after I had started work, excited word went round the office that there was going to be a Raise.

Being an indulged daughter of the middle class, I had no notions of money management, and regularly passed the last week of the month eating oatmeal, or canned soup, and walking the miles to and from work. I also used standard ploys like putting the cheque for the phone company in the envelope for the hydro and vice versa, so as to manifest my earnest intent to pay and simultaneously to defer the reality of so doing. These arrangements struck me more as amusing than anything; but the idea of More Money was very attractive.

My Raise turned out to be three dollars and seventy-five cents, gross, per month.

Miss Brewbury came into the Pit at lunchtime that day, as we ate our sandwiches (the men went out to restaurants). She explained for the benefit of "all you new people" that it was the custom there for each employee to write a little thank-you note to Mr. Elliott, the elder of the two unseen sixth-floor brothers, to express our appreciation of The Raise.

I was the only one to offer any objection to this directive, and I did so only after Miss Brewbury had left the Pit.

Mrs. Kavanagh said that young people were often ungrateful.

The young woman whose desk was next to mine on the other side said, "Maybe you got some funny ideas over at that college you went to."

A couple of the women did agree that the raises were pitiful, though to me that was not the worst of it.

When the office manager came round later in the afternoon to "collect" our notes, she checked through the pile and then stared at me. The Pit fell silent. I could not look at Miss Brewbury, but gazed at the keys of my typewriter. Finally she squeaked away. I went to the washroom and cried from fear and shame.

Some days after this episode, Miss Brewbury summoned me

to her presence and said peevishly that from now on I was assigned to Mr. Ferguson, the editor of *The Miner's Messenger*. "He says you spell well."

The Miner's Messenger was the company's flagship publication. It dated back, through a kind of apostolic succession of ownerships, to California Gold Rush days. Mr. Ferguson never spoke when he dropped his work at the Pit. Always, when the secretaries arrived in the morning, the light in his office was on and he was there, bent over his typewriter or with blue pencil in hand, and when we left in the evening, he remained.

Mr. Ferguson was, I had heard, a John Bircher. At Berkeley, students had contemptuously described and assessed the opinions of these people. Since I was proudly ignorant of all politics, I simply thought Birchers must be stupid or uneducated (I tended to confuse these two categories).

When I took Mr. Ferguson his coffee on the first morning of our association, he asked me to distinguish between the uses of *which* and *that* and to give examples.

He then explained what my work was to be. First I would learn to assemble the hired-promoted-fired-died column in *The Miner's Messenger*. In writing up this news, I was to split no infinitives, to avoid compound-complex sentences, to use appositives in preference to relative clauses in order to save words, and to avoid the passive voice unless he had explicitly required its use so as to conceal the agent of a particular act.

Giving me a stack of Dictatapes, Mr. Ferguson scrunched down again over his editing desk, which, like his typing table, faced the wall, not the window, and began to move his lips and his blue pencil. As I left his office he asked, "The niggers on campus ever try to bother you?" Shocked, I did nothing except go on walking out.

The other women in the Pit, hearing of my new duties, said "You?" or "Well!" and in one case, "Went right over BB's head, did he?" They then resumed their work.

Mr. Ferguson loved mining country. In snatches, when receiving or handing over piles of work, he talked of his years in mining exploration in Colorado and Nevada and New Mexico, of the cold dews at dawn in those bare open lands. The sky was pale, a glazed blue, like ice in sunlight. Early in the morning the rocks revealed their colours more truly, he felt, than at any other time.

A basket of small rocks stood on his desk. While Mr. Ferguson edited, he always held one in his left hand, turning and turning the little thing, drawing his calloused forefinger and big hard thumb over the gritty irregular surface, like a lover. Some of the stones sparkled between his fingers.

Mr. Ferguson loved mining, mines, miners, minerals. He loved them especially if they were American, but had an intense feeling for the work all over the world.

He loved work.

He hated Negroes, Jews, Catholics, all levels of government, and teachers, these last because they—or at least his own children's teachers—did not hate the former.

John Fitzgerald Kennedy, said Mr. Ferguson, represented everything wrong that was happening in America.

Around this time, there took place some of the big lunch-counter sit-ins organized by the Student Non-Violent Coordinating Committee. These received extensive media coverage.

Miss Brewbury said she thought these "SNICK" youngsters (her use of the acronym exuded contempt) travelling to the South would do better to stay at home and not poke their noses into other people's business.

To my fellow Pitters, all white like me, the people involved in the sit-ins were just plain awful. Mrs. Kavanagh received a Pitful of nods when she said, "All they want to do is cause trouble."

Mr. Ferguson said that the whole thing was instigated by Communist Jews.

I could not imagine "leaving everything" (question from twenty-five years later: what did I suppose I had to leave?) and travelling by bus to unknown parts of the United States, with no source of income and no address. I looked and looked at the newspaper photographs of the freedom riders, not so much the black ones as the whites. What kinds of people were these?

This question absorbed me much of the time; I lived then in a dishevelled semi-communal house whose other inhabitants approached money, food, sex, books, words, clothes, in ways that startled me.

Nor did I understand why the other women in the Pit were so standoffish since I had been assigned to Mr. Ferguson. The work was hard and I would have welcomed consultation.

Because my seventeen years of education had omitted any study of chemistry, physics, biology, or the earth sciences, I found much of *The Miner's Messenger* incomprehensible. The unfamiliar feeling upset me.

But the concise undecorated fact-packed sentences appealed to me, as did the trenchant words: slurry, aggregate, drillbit, leaching.

Dictionaries and doing research—these I did know about, and slowly the earth on which I lived began to mean more than landscape, attractive or otherwise. I discovered that I had grown up on something called the Precambrian Shield; I inquired about the composition of those soft brown hills beyond the blue or fogbound distances of San Francisco Bay.

Mr. Ferguson's pet project was a multilingual listing of common mining terms, to be published serially as special inserts in the magazine, on perforated three-hole-punched stock for easy removal and collation.

He thought that such a work would contribute to the safety and efficiency of mining and to good relations among miners from different countries. The American industry, he believed, tended to insularity; the Russians, for example, knew a hell of a lot about hard-rock mining.

He sent me out of the office, first to the Swedish and then to the Italian Consulate, to look up mining terms in the technical dictionaries in their libraries.

An utterly beautiful black Italian youth also studied in his Consulate's library, an austere and formal room, all panelling and brocade. After lunch one day, he and I fell together on to the sunlit almond-green carpet and fucked. I supposed, returning to work later, that I must have broken just about every taboo operant within these office walls. Did I smell of sex? If home had not been so far, I would have gone there first to shower. I did not meet anyone's eyes in the Pit, and stayed, unasked, well after five o'clock to finish typing word-lists.

I loved going out of the office, because I got to walk through the streets of downtown San Francisco, to see people and buildings and more people, and to observe at every intersection how the city ran downhill to the sea.

Taking different routes to and from the various consulates, I felt continually exhilarated by the presence—by being myself *in* the presence—of such masses of varied humanity; for all my life to date, I had been a student only, in educational institutions of one kind and another, among other students only.

To re-enter the stale air of the office and the claustrophobic Pit was unpleasant, the more so because my fellow-secretaries made it clear that I had lost what limited acceptance I had earlier attained. My accent was no longer of interest.

With resentful efficiency, the other women had pretty well divided up Mrs. Kavanagh's appointed work among themselves. She spent her eight hours a day, five days a week, stuffing envelopes uncomplainingly.

The monthly rhythms of *The Miner's Messenger* drove my working hours, my aching wrists, my tired eyes, as Mr. Ferguson and I proofread the thing aloud, cover to cover, including the ads.

The crisp shining advertisements for mining equipment fascinated me in their opposition to the harshness, dirt, and danger of mining itself.

Once a full-page ad for Caterpillar faced a page that included a small story about two African miners killed by a toppling Cat. I drew this juxtaposition to Mr. Ferguson's attention.

He looked back and forth between the two pages, frowning.

"That's life," he said flatly, and reinserted the sheets in the dummy. "More accurately, that's life and death." As I turned to my work again, he added, "Plenty more where those two came from."

I got up and left his office. About half an hour later, he came to the Pit and asked me please to return. I did. This was now routine; sometimes I walked out of his office four or five times in a day.

Mr. Ferguson said, after one of these episodes, "I'd heard you had strong opinions." I did not like the pleasure I felt on hearing this.

On a November morning, we women were all in the Pit, working. Our umbilical Dictaphone cords were attached to our heads and we sat in our rows and typed away like billy-o. Suddenly Miss Brewbury came towards us, walking quickly, squeaking madly—but her face, her face! Mushroom had bleached to palest grey, plump cheeks had fallen in. In her open mouth, the dentures angled down.

Knowing instantly that Miss Brewbury would announce disaster, we snatched our hands from the keys and ripped the cords from our heads.

Even before she reached the Pit, the men were starting to come out of their office, such was the atmosphere the woman generated as she walked.

"The President has been shot. Shot. He is dying."

Later I found myself in an empty editorial office, looking out over the distant hills, the Bay, the waterfront, the downtown streets of the beautiful city.

Clusters of humans formed down there. In front of the grimy store where second-hand TVs were sold, by the doors of Fosters' restaurant, at the corner newsstand, crowds were coming into being.

A *Chronicle* truck rushed down the street, bumping over the potholes, and the boy hanging on at the back swung out a tall stack of papers. The top half of the front page was black with two gigantic lines of type: DYING IN DALLAS! EXCLUSIVE INSIDE!

The people, the newspaper: a pull as strong as gravity's took me, and I headed back through the long office towards the elevator.

Some of my fellow workers still cried quietly at their desks, while some clustered round the radio in the *Pacific Fish* editorial office. Others talked on the phone to spouses or friends with access to a TV.

"Going *out?*" asked a secretary.

"S'okay, she's Canadian, she won't feel the same," said another.

Mr. Ferguson, I saw, was working. His short chunky shape was, as usual, hunched over the old manual typewriter he had refused to exchange for a spanking new IBM ("Impossible man!" said Miss Brewbury). He was beating some article into submission and pretending nothing had happened. I stuck my head into his office.

"You know the President of the United States is dead."

"Good," said Mr. Ferguson.

The air in the street was shockingly fresh, clear.

I bought the paper. Photographs of President Kennedy, Mrs. Kennedy, the Kennedy children, Kennedy associates, and the Kennedy extended family in all its extant generations, plus Joe—these filled the bottom half of the first page and all of the second. The rest of the newspaper was exactly what I'd skimmed that morning, even to a full itinerary for JFK's day in Dallas.

"And I bought this?" I flung it on the street. The face was uppermost; I looked down at that self-consciously presented profile, that spurious nobility (for no child of Ontario's establishment could be much impressed by this leader of a *republic*).

Yet the assassination terrified me. Where could I go, what do?

Looking up, I saw that more people were gathering about me.

Where did they end? There were so many—I had never seen so many in one place. They were quiet, or they conversed in low tones, telling each other where they had been, what doing, when the news came to them. Because they wanted to be with each other, they came out into the street, and more still came, from the offices and warehouses and towers. Afraid of what was happening in the country where they lived, they knew that with each other they would not be so afraid. Among them were the assistant circulation manager of *Fertilizing California Today* and a couple of guys from Accounting. We waved.

In the street, among these hundreds and thousands, I felt like more than a solitary self, and this new feeling poured through me like the strength of streams of water over raw ore.

Returning to the office, I saw Mr. Ferguson's blue pencil still moving along the lines, darting at waste and clumsiness and error.

I went eagerly to the women in the Pit.

Design and Spontaneity

The prospect from the Mortimers' living-room was grey: sky, trees, hard-crusted snow.

To get the yellow linen of the curtains in view, Julian moved back. He stood at the more northern of the two windows. From the street, however, it would appear that a teenage boy stood at the middle one of three. The Mortimers' apartment comprised the upper floors of an old house, the conversion of which had blocked off a small windowed area, accessible now only through the closet in Mr. Mortimer's study and fitted with a pair of curtains matching those in the living-room.

Julian was on a bored Sunday-evening lookout for B. K. Beardsley, an English academic editor. Mr. Mortimer had shown his son a letter from this unknown scholar. "See that handwriting, Julian? What d'you call that? A strong fair hand. Where'd BKB learn to write like that? Why, in Britain, of course. Look at your handwriting. Look at your mother's. Look at mine. Sloppy, characterless, ill-formed. And where did we learn to write? Why, in Canada," and Mr. Mortimer took the bristly black script away to appreciate further.

No sound. No people. No taxi yet: Uncle Webby and Mrs. T always arrived thus. Back in the dining-room—*clink clink*—

Mrs. Mortimer was tipping horse-radish into its blue-lined silver bowl. Now she would hum back to the kitchen. And down from the third floor came Mr. Mortimer, quick *one*-two, *one*-two; checked his grey tie in the hallway mirror; peered—Julian saw perfectly through the back of his head—down the passage to ensure that the lavatory door was slightly open; adjusted the velvet curtain concealing the dumb-waiter; and stepped briskly into the dining-room.

"Meredith, what have you done? B. K. Beardsley and the three of us—why six places?"

The wooden spoon knocked against the roaster as Mrs. Mortimer spooned up hot bloody fat. "It's the last Sunday of the month, Timothy. Their chamber music concert."

Around the street corner came a small woman in a bright red coat.

"My God, Meredith, why didn't you put them off?"

"We never do, Timothy."

The red woman created a quick purposeful centre of attention in the grey. She looked from house to house.

"Why does this have to happen?" Gesticulating, Mr. Mortimer entered the living-room. "These blasted people aren't even related to me by blood. Aunt Alison died thirty years ago—why aren't you helping your mother?—Uncle Esmond died twenty-eight years ago—what are you gawking at? My father's in-laws." He reached the window.

Julian went to the kitchen. It was in utter order. Smiling, Mrs. Mortimer poked toothpicks through cheese canapes.

"Now who's this red woman? Another guest of yours, Meredith? No sarcasm intended, you understand, but who is she?"

"I have no idea, dear."

Returning to the living-room, Julian collided with his father, bent on an urgent exit.

"Well, she'll have to be told to go away, won't she? Suppose she's a Witness?" Mr. Mortimer was bounding downstairs to the apartment door, which opened on the house's great front hall. "Suppose she's still here when BKB arrives, yammering about blood transfusions or redemption? Fine impression that'll make, won't it?"

Julian saw the blue snout of a taxi. "Uncle Webby and Mrs. T are here."

Mr. Mortimer banged the apartment door after him, as if determined that no scarlet woman should gain access. "Dear Mrs. T, dear to me." Mrs. Mortimer carried in sherry-glasses. "Webby looked even frailer than usual last time."

"Mum, you say those two things every single solitary month."

"Do I? Well, they're true."

"B. K. Beardsley!" shouted Mr. Mortimer below. The red woman had got into the hall. Inside the taxi, Mrs. T pointed with her fold-up cane and opened her purse. The doorbell's ring indicated that Mr. Mortimer had forgotten his key. Julian ran down to open. Smiling, the woman held out her hand. His father coughed. "Dr. Beardsley, my son, Julian."

"Bessie, please."

"Bessie? Bessie? Very well, upstairs, can you see?"

A shirred lace curtain veiled the oval glass in the front door, obscuring the human shapes on the sidewalk outside.

"Hi Uncle Webby, hi Mrs. T," said Julian, opening. "Was the concert good?"

"The Mozart wasn't," said Mrs. T with her brilliant lips.

"My boy, the Mozart was *not*." Short Uncle Webby, supported by tall Mrs. T, waved one of his canes emphatically.

"Webster, concentrate!" Mrs. T's single cane nosed at the shallow steps. Julian got on Webby's other side and helped heave up his pillowy frame, swathed in a grey mohair shawl.

"They changed the program, Julian. Look. In my pocket."

"Not *now*, Webby. Julian's going to hold the door."

"Wolfgang Amadeus Mozart. Sonata for Violin and Piano in B flat major. Kirchel 378." Triumphantly, "How's that for an old man?" as they achieved the front hall. "Oh— that climb!" In an urgent shuffle Uncle Webby reached a chair by the hall table, where a tall Chinese vase erupted in chrysanthemums.

"To paint that colour . . . " said Mrs. T, stroking a shaggy bundle.

"Look, Julian. *After* the Haydn. *Before* the Mendelssohn: the Mozart. And they made a substitution! Julian, when the announcement was made, a *frisson* swept through the recital hall. A shiver. A —"

"*Frissons* don't sweep, Webby. Here. Smell." Mrs. T took a flower and held the bitter wet bloom under her relatives' noses. "The musicians were excited. Shostakovitch. They wanted to share. With their devoted audience. Altogether reasonable."

"No, Mrs. T!" Uncle Webby tapped his two canes on the floor. "Devotion, excitement—singly or together, they are simply inadequate to justify such a change. Let us first consider *devotion*. I am myself devoted, but—"

"Webby. Up." Mrs. T replaced the flower.

"But to presume upon that devotion is elitist," explained Uncle Webby, as Julian hauled him to his feet again. "And unprofessional. New audience members undoubtedly felt excluded by this familial informality." Mrs. T took up a severely waiting attitude by the Mortimers' apartment door. "And in addition they felt, I am sure, offended. Disappointed." Julian drew back the leather curtain that concealed the dumb-waiter and manoeuvred Uncle Webby in. He pulled the rope. "Unreliability—*that* is what such a substitution signals, to a newcomer." Uncle Webby, his voice resonating in the shaft, slowly disappeared.

"Shostakovitch. Execrable. No other word." Mrs. T preceded her great-nephew up the nineteen stairs. "Much admired. Earlier in this century. Siege of Leningrad. Admirable, no doubt." She was now on stair fourteen. From the apartment hallway above, the dumb-waiter clicked its arrival. No voices sounded. "No musicality whatsoever. And we might have had the Mozart!" Mrs. T stepped up into the silence where Bessie Beardsley smiled as Mr. Mortimer drew back the bulging velvet.

"Aha, Mrs. T!" cried Uncle Webby. "You admit it! To jettison the Mozart was an error."

Mrs. Mortimer emerged from the kitchen, carrying a cut-glass dish of hot toasted almonds rolled in salt.

"Timothy, what are you thinking of? Introductions. Julian, help Webby. Dr. Beardsley, Bessie, a nut. Mrs. T, my dear, it seems more than a month, I do like that dress, wonderful peacock blue. Bessie Beardsley, Mrs. T, my aunt by marriage. A nut? Bessie Beardsley, Webster Willoughby, my uncle by marriage. The living-room, a glass of sherry, a nut, do . . . ."

At the eastern head of his table, Mr. Mortimer aimed his carving knife straight through the animal. "Shall we all hear now from Bessie, on her impressions? The flight? Her recapitulation, so much swifter than our forbears could have dreamed, of their journeys? The sword of the ice-blue river aimed at the heart of the country?"

"You know my stomach, Timothy," said Uncle Webby, confidingly. "I trust there will be no surprises."

"Your digestive tract is surely familiar by now with roast beef and two veg," said Mrs. T, between uncle and niece.

Smiling calmly at the western foot, Mrs. Mortimer indicated to her son, on her left, that he should start the gravy-boat.

"Liquid satin!" Bessie Beardsley took two ladlesful. Behind thick glasses, her blue eyes shone.

All seemed intolerably tedious and grotesque to Julian, whose mother was always asking why he didn't bring his friends home more often.

"It is best to alternate mouthfuls of the different foods on one's plate." With his knife, Uncle Webby made a delicate clockwise movement. "Doing so facilitates digestion."

"Rubbish," snapped Mr. Mortimer.

"Fortunately," Webby continued, "dear Meredith's cooking makes duty a pleasure. Rich, mind you"—he twirled a thickly-buttered Brussels sprout in his gravy—"but I find that *well*-cooked rich food presents no problem to my system. Greasy foods, however, though I take all pains to avoid them—"

"Web, why don't you ever take a scientific approach?"

"Science, Timothy, has been slow to perceive the natural laws relating to the ingestion of foodstuffs. We now know . . . ."

"Why shouldn't our taste-buds have whatever they want next?"

"What is it like to fly over the North Pole?" inquired Mrs. T of Bessie Beardsley. The blue eyes of the stranger considered.

"In a way, Mrs. T, it's like flying over an idea. There's nothing to *see*. The pilot simply announces the proximity of the Pole, below. The flight attendants point."

"And the passengers simply believe."

"Yes . . . . A reality is there, of course, beyond that funny thick glass. Otherwise the plane would not be flying."

"Of course." Mrs. T drank burgundy. "But you do see the continent, when you get that far? You see vast North America?"

The guest opened her eyes wide. "Vaster than imagination."

"To you, certainly, in comparison to the U.K."

"I was born here. This is home."

"That explains your accent." Mrs. T raised her glass again. Bessie Beardsley smiled at her.

Julian waited, seething, for his father to resume carving.

"You don't need to be formal about inviting friends," his mother said. "You could just ask someone home after school."

He rolled his eyes at her. "I don't do things on impulse."

"Then you could choose someone, and ask him in advance. For dinner next Friday, say."

"If I asked anyone on Monday, then by Friday I'd wish he wasn't coming."

Lifting her serving spoons, Mrs. Mortimer turned to Mrs. T. "It should be man-woman all round the table, I know, but Web has nothing to say to *me*. I wanted to be next to you."

Mrs. T wistfully raised her glass. "Meredith, what does this woman want with Timothy?"

"Oh . . . an article of his. One of those titles with a colon. A magazine." Mrs. Mortimer saw her husband hold his knife and fork still as he listened to Bessie. "How was your concert?"

"There was a substitution. Unexpected." Mrs. T laughed. "These afternoons—Webby and I. His canes, and difficulties. The other regulars. All that white hair, or no hair. The familiar pieces, after a quarter-century. Startling!" Both laughed.

Webby had almost finished his second helping of everything. Staring, Julian counted the chews for each mouthful, adding up, taking an average, as Webby set down his knife and fork, precisely north-south. Cruelty formed on the boy's face. His mouth opened.

"Julian," said Mrs. Mortimer sharply, "go and draw the living-room curtains. Have we all finished? Shall we clear?"

By covering the cold window glass, Julian shut out the grey and created two vivid yellow oblongs. Then he went to his father's study and through the closet to the window room, where he made another oblong and lay down on the floor, head to the south. Under his grey sweater, the floor was cold. The dark silence soothed him. The neurotic obsessions of these adults and the imminence of school became unreal.

Bessie had listened attentively to Mr. Mortimer. "You feel that most academics write poorly."

"What else is there to feel? Doctoral students in literature elect to write on Peacock, Austen, Sterne. They choose those wonderful stylists—clear as crystal—why choose them, if not for love? And what do these students write, then? Bleary, cloudy, lumpy, meaningless prose."

"So love may not mean understanding or ability to emulate."

"Do you see any love in the theses you edit? Where is love? Suffocated under sixty-seven-word sentences. Why can't they write plain English? What's stopping them? What good is love if it produces travesty? I'll get my paper." He rose. She rose.

Mrs. Mortimer and Mrs. T removed the debris of the first course to the kitchen and companionably set about recreating order.

Webby kept his solitary post at the dinner-table. A certain cut-glass dish was absent from the sideboard: might there be trifle? The early stages of his digestion felt smooth.

Voices sounded in the study. "You see I used *Journey*. Is that the best? *Quest? Pilgrimage?*"

"They are more passionate," said Bessie Beardsley, "if passion is what you want." Flap flap of pages turning.

"Julian should crumb the table." His mother crossed the hall to her husband's study. "What has become of Julian?"

The lamplight winked on the frames of their glasses as Mr. Mortimer and Bessie regarded the stapled sheaf of papers.

"How should I know, my dear? Has he vanished?"

"I sent him to draw the curtains. Oh."

"Aha!" cried Mr. Mortimer, moving rapidly. Light burst into the window-room. "Discovered!" Bessie Beardsley smiled.

"Where is everyone?" called Webby.

"Julian, one simply does *not* disappear at a dinner-party. Now go and crumb the table. Dessert is ready. We're all coming, Webby. The article, Bessie, later? Mrs. T, watch that rug, the fringe sticks up. Timothy, the switch on the coffee-pot. Now!"

Toasted coconut bordered the trifle's cloak of cream. The jam, under the rich yellow emulsion, was unexpectedly rhubarb.

"The coconut is not traditionally English, I know," said Mrs. Mortimer, serving Bessie generously, "but *we* like it."

Mrs. T was the first to lay down her spoon. "Webby. Not *per se* an error. The change in the program."

Mr. Mortimer's "Tsk!" was explosive. "Come come, Mrs. T! This can't possibly interest our guest."

"Timothy, my dear, the head and the heart—the old tussle. What would you say to that, Bessie?"

"I would like to hear more."

Mrs. Mortimer, about to offer seconds, put down the serving spoon. Julian and Webby sighed.

"The musicians today," Mrs. T said with authority, "changed *their* program. Much surprise, and disapproval too"—Webby nodded hard—"but. Correct. They acted out of love." Mrs. T drank, and her wig twitched. "Their joy in Shostakovitch—obvious. Their music. They made it. Not us. As for us—we'd freely elected to come and hear . . . "

"Not *free*," Webby interjected. "Season's tickets. Went up this year, *again*. Well over—"

"Hush, Web," said Mr. and Mrs. Mortimer.

" . . . to come and hear them, we cannot criticize their spur-of-the-moment decision to give themselves the pleasure of playing for us what pleased them." Mrs. T emptied her glass.

"Can I have some more trifle, Mum?"

Bessie Beardsley asked, "What did you think of the Shostakovitch, Mrs. T?"

"But its quality isn't the point at issue, now is it?"—Mr. Mortimer violently scraped his dessert-plate—"No no, the issue is order against anarchy, isn't it? Or shall we say reason and passion? The established and the unpredictable? Even sense and sensibility?"

"Oh, the thing was all wrong," declared Webby. "Ill-mannered. Presumptuous. But the music! May I have a little more trifle, Meredith? The Shostakovitch—wonderful!"

"Dreadful!" cried Mrs. T.

Bessie Beardsley laughed. Mrs. Mortimer laughed, and dealt big spoonfuls.

"Wonderful," repeated Webby. "At first, you understand, the ear doubts. *Can this sound be? Is this rhythm?* But then! A little more coconut, please."

"Chamber-music concerts—one doesn't go there for unfamiliarity," said Mrs. T. "No thank you Meredith, delicious."

"Where *do* you go for unfamiliarity, Mrs. T?" Bessie, nodding to Mrs. Mortimer's inquiring eye, passed her plate.

"Long ago, married twice," Mrs. T responded. "Many other men, afterwards."

"Mrs. T!" exclaimed all her relatives except Julian.

"And now?" asked Bessie Beardsley.

"Paintings. Not painters. I get drunk on paint."

"Julian, go and get the coffee tray."

"I married Eric Turner very soon after Esmond died. I'd been so happy. After Eric died too, I saw actual *marriage* wasn't required. The form."

Mrs. Mortimer stirred her coffee. "Bessie, what do you do for unfamiliarity?"

"I leave my house and go walking in the city," the guest

immediately answered, her voice warm with enthusiasm. "I look at people, and in apartment windows, and at houses— other ways of arranging life."

"Oh my . . . to do that in London . . . ." Mrs. Mortimer looked faraway.

"The man who is tired of London is tired of life," offered Webby. "The woman too," affably.

Mr. Mortimer gave an exasperated sigh. "Webby, *When* a man is tired of London, he is etcetera.' Johnson."

Some time after the party's transfer to the living-room, the host excused himself. A little later, when Julian touched the lavatory door, he caught sight of his father still in the dim bathroom, before the mirror. Mr. Mortimer had taken off his glasses. With a damp washcloth, he wiped and wiped his eyes. "My article," he murmured, wiping, and he supported himself with his other hand on the sink. Rattling the knob, Julian went in to the toilet.

When he returned to the living-room, Mr. Mortimer was gesturing vehemently. "Web, how can you cherish reliability and still welcome the Shostakovitch?"

"Sound is not something I eat," stated Webby, and sipped his Irish Cream. "It is not a busy street I must cross. It is not an intruder with hostile intent at the window of my little apartment. There is no danger, with sound."

"Paint is different, then," declared Mrs. T. "Most powerful. Like flying. Seeing the world new." She drank her brandy down.

"My God, woman, what about words? Do you dare to rank paint as more powerful than words?"

"Acting may be the most powerful of all," Mrs. Mortimer said. She and her husband were drinking her home-made raspberry liqueur.

"*I* think film has them all beat." Julian reached for the Irish Cream.

"Acting?" asked Bessie Beardsley. "How so, Meredith?"

"Because even when an actor has a familiar script, even when the whole audience knows and loves the play, everything is still unpredictable. A person can completely change familiar meaning." Mrs. Mortimer smiled warmly at her family and guest. "Like a menu in the window of a restaurant with a new chef."

"What about dance? Hey, what about dance?" Grinning, Julian reached again.

But everyone else was too old and full. A feeling of closure had come.

"Well—" said Bessie. She and Webby and Mrs. T all rose. Assembled in the dark chill downstairs, five people inhaled chrysanthemums and watched Webby hatch out of the dumbwaiter.

Bessie began shaking hands all round. "I'm glad, Timothy, that I was there when you discovered Julian. Otherwise I would have had to *ask* for an explanation of the third yellow window."

"You noticed!" cried Julian.

"So that was why," said Mrs. Mortimer and Mrs. T.

"The yellow looked so vivid. So inviting." Bessie Beardsley smiled at the men. "Everything else—grey. And I was cold. I thought, 'Someone who would choose bright yellow curtains—worth meeting. An interesting arrangement.' So."

"Do you mean to say you're not B. K. Beardsley? What about my article? Where is he?"

"My name *is* Bessie." She shook Mr. Mortimer's hand.

Uncle Webby chuckled. "A two-surprise day! And, as always, a wonderful dinner." He kissed his niece.

Mrs. T gave a chrysanthemum to Bessie. So did Mrs. Mortimer. "Safe home," she said, opening the glass door. "Here's the taxi."

"But where is *he*, Meredith?"

"Maybe his plane was late, Timothy love. Listen—there's the phone."

Mr. Mortimer took the stairs two at a time. Julian leapt after him, hearing the call of the fallen trifle. Contentedly, Mrs. Mortimer closed her apartment door.

Gold, Silver, Ivory, Slate, and Wood

Even out in the hot country, in the great empty provinces and states that towered and rolled and sloped and stretched from coast to coast, in the huge landscapes where the tour coach buzzed across flat terrain like the needle of a sewing-machine across a giant sheet—even there, hundreds of people were always around whenever they stopped at an attraction. Often it was hard for Ray to get a good picture. And the urban crowds of tourists were terrible.

Once Edie fainted in the heat. This was on their last morning in New York. The bus—not the friendly tour coach, just a regular city bus—was lurching up Fifth Avenue. The vehicle and the street and the sidewalks were crammed. Edie slumped over on to Ray. Tiffany's was to the right—Edie was missing it! Ray looked around but no face of any age or colour showed recognition of his difficulty. Edie's mouth opened. Was she going to be sick? He must get her head down, restore the blood. Awkwardly he manoeuvred himself sideways. The bus jolted. Edie's head fell heavily on to his thighs. Her glasses went askew and the riders stuck up through her grey hair like antlers. Ray took off the glasses and pushed Edie over so her head hung between her knees. Her summer dress stretched thin over the straps of her bra and lace-trimmed slip. Through the fabric he saw several moles, close together: a brown snowflake. He had not noticed that in years. By the upper sixties he judged it was safe for them to get off the bus, find a taxi.

Back at the hotel, Edie said she wanted to take a turn around the block, to get some air. Ray agreed, though he was worried about checkout time, about getting on the tour bus. Of course he had his arm firmly under Edie's, was steering. A light shower came. The warm drops might mean thunder; how would it be for them, riding the bus in a storm? Ray saw his wife turn her head upwards and smile as the water fell on her cheeks, on her pearl necklace. He was tired, or something—he would be glad to get back into the dry. He felt funny, not really funny—he could not find other terms. Ray wanted to hurry.

In their room, after Edie had rested while he packed up, and then washed her face and tidied her hair, she said, "Ray, my glasses?" He could not remember. He checked his pockets. Polishing his own glasses, he reviewed events. He had not thought to take the number of the bus, the cab. So the glasses were gone. Then Edie did what Ray always found so irritating.

"I'll be fine," she said.

But their extra medical insurance was designed to smooth out just such mishaps. She could visit a New York optometrist; they could stay in the city a day or so longer, to get the new glasses, and join the next Travellers' Joy tour.

Edie said, "I don't want to meet a whole lot of strangers on another tour. I like the people we're with now."

Ray did not share her sentiment. And if they had taken any other Travellers' Joy tour, say the preceding or the following one, wouldn't Edie have liked the people on it too? But he saw that her feeling was strong. He did not speak his thought.

He moved to his next argument: a principal reason for travelling, especially on a cross-continental bus tour, was to *see* things.

"I'll see," Edie said matter-of-factly. "It's just a bit blurry is all. Kind of nice actually. Like those French impressionists in Texas or Arizona or wherever they were."

The diagnosis of Edie's MS had come shortly before the three great events: their thirtieth wedding anniversary; Ray's retirement, after almost four decades, from the shoe store; and the commencement of the trip. The doctor's words shocked. Yet Ray felt also the calm coincident with anticipated disaster. Edie had always been frail and he robust. He was accustomed to the necessity of sparing her, would simply have to spare her more. And Edie was surely enjoying herself on this trip. "We're seeing so much, Ray," she kept saying, "I never knew, did you?" Unlike many of the other passengers, she did not each day refer more often to the happiness of going home.

Probably, Ray thought, his insides would feel better once he got there.

Pearls were the gift for a thirtieth anniversary (Ray had checked the almanac). He had considered giving Edie a pearl ring, but in recent years her fingers had begun to warp with arthritis. He looked at brooches, scarfpins, bracelets, earrings. Eventually he chose a necklace. The graduated order of the pearls satisfied him, although the clasp had to be changed, for in Ray's experience a pair of interlocking circles was harder to fasten than a small shaft, like a tiny hairpin, that slid tightly into a holder. He operated the substituted clasp a number of times before paying for the present.

"Mild," said Dr. Spokes repeatedly after giving Ray and Edie the diagnosis, "mild." He talked about gradual change and said, "Have a good trip. You've both earned it."

In Ray's opinion, Edie ought not to wear the pearls all the time. He had told her so the morning after the anniversary party, at the breakfast table. Pearls did not go with housecoats, or woolly sweaters, or bright cotton summer prints.

"Ray, they feel warm on me. If I take them off, they're all cold when I put them on again." Edie kissed him on the cheek.

To Ray, "gradual" was not the right word for the changes in his wife. Edie's energy lessened sharply. During the spring planting she did only the bedding plants, which always went into window boxes. She did not bend or kneel or carry, but stayed on the wicker settee on the front porch, holding the boxes on her lap and arranging the pink petunias next to the white and then the purple, as always. When she had finished, Ray took the heavy rectangles of earth and fitted them into their wire holders. He did all the basket planters and hung them up. He did the standing planters by the walk in the back yard too, because Edie said she was tired now. If she kept going down at this rate . . . ?

Daily, after breakfast, the two checked on the marigolds, alyssum, lobelias, Edie exclaiming with pleasure as the minute green frills and points emerged from the dark earth. Ray was annoyed if all the plants did not germinate, after his careful sifting and sowing and hardening. He moved one of the garden chairs to the end of the walk, by the back fence, so Edie could rest before they started back to the house for their second cup of coffee.

In the brief weeks between the diagnosis and the trip, Ray inquired repeatedly of Edie, "How do you feel? How are you feeling today?"

"Oh all right," she might say, or, "I think I'll have a little rest before I start supper." She might even go on to some other subject. "How often do you think Evelyn will need to water when we're on the trip?" Evelyn was their daughter; she and her husband had given Ray and Edie their anniversary party. Somehow Evelyn had tracked down people unseen for years— former neighbours and bridge partners and fellow bowlers. "It brings it all back, doesn't it, Ray?" Edie kept asking him during the party, flushed with celebration, the pearls gleaming on the silky blue of her new best dress. Ray supposed that was true, though he had not missed anyone. She was exhausted the next day. Evelyn had not allowed for that. When he had tidied up the party debris that his daughter had missed, Ray checked the hoses and the sprinkler, and polished the small brass watering can they used for the house plants.

Before their trip, Ray made time to visit a medical supplies store and measure wheelchairs. Then he checked the whole house. Fortunately these solid old houses, even the small ones, had wide doors. He would need to move the refrigerator and build a lower counter. The bathroom would accommodate a wheelchair, leaving easy room for him to install handrails. The only problem was the door to his and Edie's bedroom, or rather the cramped hallway off which the doors to bedrooms and bath opened. Ray remembered Edie commenting on the awkward layout when Evelyn was small and her belongings lay about. The child had learned to be tidy. Ray saw now that an adjustment could readily be made which would also take an odd jog out of the wall of their room. Two for the price of one. He thought about carpenters. A while off. Still, better to plan. That left only the matter of a ramp to either the front or the back porch. Not easy; Ray took measurements, made sketches to scale. He could train climbing vines up the side of the ramp, roses perhaps, Algerian ivy. He did not discuss any of this with Edie.

On the first night of Ray and Edie's anniversary and retirement trip, the silk flowers in the lobby of the Travellers' Rest drew much comment. Everyone was tired, for even a luxury coach, with air conditioning and reclining seats and well-PineSoled toilet, becomes uncomfortable after hours of sitting and watching the passage of unfamiliar territory, landscape bluish round the edges of cold windows. All the passengers got stiffly down into the sunset warmth and walked to the glowing Dining Room sign (Ray took a picture of the place before he and Edie entered). Looking with interest about the lobby, the group saw and then looked more closely at and then felt the lilies, azaleas, roses. A wife exclaimed, "Amazing!" Other female voices joined in—So much better than that stiff shiny plastic, no maintenance, no bugs, such a good idea, so fresh, pretty. Ray thought the flowers were sensible, for a public place. Edie said, "They don't smell," and the tour guide motioned them forward into the restaurant.

Here were their reserved tables. How pleasant it was to have travel arrangements made by someone else! Edie had suggested that they just wander about Canada and the States on their own, but Ray was sure that for them an arranged tour would be better. Edie's illness was the confirmation. Now, as directed, they sat with another couple, to get acquainted. A coincidence: this wife had first exclaimed at the silk flowers, and she, with her

husband, sat in the seat right in front of Ray and Edie in the
bus. (By a logic unclear to Ray, this other husband and wife
thereafter sat next them at each Travellers' Rest dinner of the
tour.) Edie and the other wife chatted with capable enthusiasm.
The waitress came with the big plastic-coated menus, written in flowing script, and moments later she was back with big
glasses of ice water. Everything sounded so good. They con-
sulted, decided, changed their minds, finally ordered. Then,
almost before the couples had had time to hear each other's
names and provenances, their food arrived. Such excellent service! Such big portions! The food was heaped on big oval plates,
almost platters. So generous. How could they finish? The coffee
was fresh and strong, even though they knew that Sanka was
better for them. Then another tour arrived, crowding into the
lobby and exclaiming at the silk plants, and there was their guide
signalling. Just time to visit the bright clean washrooms with
their shining tiles. What a pleasant interlude . . . .

Often on the tour they would stay in motels, for many of
the Travellers' Rest franchises featured accommodations, but
the first night of travel was to be spent sleeping as the bus rolled
through the dark. Ray and Edie settled in, feeling adventurous,
together, shoes off and fleecy slippers on, waistbands loosened,
warm sweaters added, cushions beneath their heads, and on their
laps the light mohair blankets that Evelyn's bridge group had
given them for the trip. "The girls spent too much, Ray. But
aren't they beautiful?" The other husband and the other wife
admired the blankets too.

Edie went to sleep first, as she had done all their thirty years
together. The bus groaned on to the dark approach ramp, and
Ray saw the driver shift into high gear and settle into his chair
as one who plans to sit just so for hours.

Lying beside Edie, all those years, Ray had usually thought
about what he was going to do the next day: take inventory,
place orders, redo the displays in the store windows, show a
new salesman how to fit a difficult foot and—as important—
how to make the customer feel that her foot was not difficult
but special . . . .

He wished the sound of the bus would vary, but the freeway ran flat and straight and the steady thrumming continued. Now Ray did not know what he would do tomorrow. On this tour, of course, he would sit each day, and get out of the bus several times to eat or to see things close up. What those things would be, he wasn't quite sure. Edie's sleep was gentle as always. Of course—tomorrow he would take pictures. All through the trip he would take pictures. At last he was to have the time, real time, to enjoy his photography. That was what he would do. What kinds of pictures should he take, now? How best to remember this journey? He turned to Edie, and the pearls shone round her neck. Small sounds broke through those of the engine and the airconditioning: snores, occasional whispers, grunts as people sought comfort in the fat chairs. The pearls were globules of blue milk in the semi-dark.

Eventually Ray slept that night, but the Travellers' Rest food weighed on him and he woke frequently, only once sensing that he had been deeply under. Dreams had been in him, something about scarlet water. His body did not feel customary. Yet he was not nauseated. He did not think diarrhea was developing. This wasn't the flu. He could not name his sensation. It was as if things inside were softening. He watched Edie. In their little pair of seats, it was almost as if they were alone together.

At dawn the noise of the bus stopped at last, at another Travellers' Rest. The air outside was fresh, dewy. They were among mountains. The sky was bright. All else—lobby, plants, menus, ice-water, portions, coffee, washrooms, crowds—was the same. To Ray, Edie looked pale. When she went into the restaurant washroom, he felt as if he were saying goodbye to her; when he went into the Men's, the gleam on the tiles and the bright fluorescents and the chrome suggested a mortuary.

Edie seemed, returning, to place her feet oddly as she walked. After thirty-seven years in the shoe store, Ray knew feet. Most of the travellers on this tour were poorly shod, although he would not tell them so, had learned decades ago not to waste his time. But the irritation remained. Too many women parcelled their plump arthritic feet into high wedges or strappy sandals. Then they complained. The other wife was a perfect example, as he pointed out to Edie. Men tended to be more sensible. Still, too many slopped about in those loose loafers that gave no support—for instance, the other husband, who also claimed to be a photographer, although Ray had only a few times seen him with camera to eye. Ray himself wore solid cotton canvas deck shoes with a built-in arch support and a Dr. Scholl's insole on top of that. And cotton socks, cotton. Feet breathe.

Maybe this odd walk was the next phase of Edie's illness? He asked her repeatedly, as the days and weeks of the trip passed, "Do your feet hurt?" "Oh Ray, it's just a little ache. We walked a lot today, in that gallery. Wasn't it wonderful?" He felt her feet all over, thoroughly, and she did not wince.

Now they were not all that far from home—up through the rest of New York state, and then just part of Canada to cross. Dr. Spokes could advise. He might have suggestions, explanations. Ray's feet never hurt. (His knees sometimes did, after all those years of kneeling to customers.) He and Edie got an excellent discount at the store. He had bought the deck shoes there, had a good chat with the boys. Edie chose two nice pairs of Naturalizers. How long would she use them? Ray thought back to the retirement cities they had seen in the sunbelt of the American south. Edie had disliked them. "There are no children," she pointed out. What Ray saw there was the solitary men who walked fat or withered dogs. Cigarettes lay on these men's lips, inhaled down to the filters so smoke curled right up their nostrils and into their eyes as they stood on corners waiting for the tour bus to groan past. The dogs sat down wearily beside them or shivered up against their masters' pantlegs.

In the museums and galleries on the tour, Edie always noticed children and animals in the paintings, sculptures, mosaics that the docents showed them. These buildings—Ray had not imagined there were so many on the continent, just as he had never imagined the continent itself was still on the whole so empty—of course held other things besides works of art. However, Ray often did not see why people had bothered to keep so many objects from the past. Poorly designed and ill made in the first place, they lay botched and battered on the shelves. Inadequate labelling often prevented him from understanding their uses.

Soon Ray took to leaving the group, on entering one of these places, to tour quickly through and gain an overall impression. If nothing interested him, he went out on the steps—most museums had broad long steps offering a good prospect of some central urban scene—and took pictures. Unlike many photographers on the trip, he never sought others' opinions on aperture or angles.

Ray thought his collection would represent the trip well. In addition to photographing every attraction visited, he had taken pictures of all the "Welcome To____" signs they had encountered, in daylight anyway: cities, states, hamlets, provinces, wildlife preserves, resorts, capitals, national parks, historic sites and monuments. At home he would arrange these in the albums, as a guide, for he hated it when people he knew showed their pictures and asked each other, "Dear, do you remember where this was?" Where possible, Ray had also photographed the official flowers, birds, and animals of the various jurisdictions, and if unable to do so he had bought postcards. At Edie's request, he took some photos of their travelling companions and appeared in some of theirs.

One great museum offered a large exhibit of Indian art from the Pacific Northwest and also—or was it at another? after weeks of travel Ray would have to check his diary—galleries of French impressionists. He had not seen anything like these Indian objects, though there must be places back home in Vancouver where such works were kept. They were puzzling, but intricate, ingenious; the design elements interconnected so that Ray wanted to follow a line from beginning back to beginning. An accompanying text—for once, clear and full—informed him that the Haida worked in gold, silver, ivory, slate, and wood. Examples were nearby. Wood: the large flat eyes on the poles were strange to Ray. Were they closed or open? There did not appear to be pupils, yet the eyes looked. The text referred to visions and dreams.

Among the other artifacts, the bent-corner cedar boxes from Bella Bella fascinated Ray. Repeatedly, he read about the heating and the kerfing and the storage of daylight in such a box. The Tlingit baskets of watertight woven spruceroot also earned Ray's unstinted admiration. "Isn't that something," he said to Edie, several times. "That's really something." He bought post-cards showing all these works.

Edie chose a sheaf of Impressionists, watery flowery shapes wavering into one another, irradiated with quivering light. Sitting on the bus, she held these up close to her eyes and went through the set again and again, smiling. Pissarro's dots made Ray's eyes water, although the theory behind them interested him as a photographer, and when all was said and done he thought Manet and Monet and the rest were out of focus. Edie had excitedly brought him to a painting in which a woman wore a necklace like hers, ordered pearls of milky blue—but, as Ray pointed out to her, you could hardly tell where one pearl stopped and the next started. She bought several postcards of this painting anyway.

Waking one night in the artificial cool of a Travellers' Rest somewhere on the eastern seaboard, Ray settled down again after swallowing a couple of Tums and checking Edie in the other twin bed. Closing his eyes felt good, the touch of one lid to the other. Those Indian eyes, if open, had seen a lot he never had. Strange to think that he and the people who made those things lived on the same continent. If he were back in the museum perhaps he could touch one of those eyes, stroke across lid or ball . . . . In that painting, the pearls were almost the same colour as the woman's skin, lacking only its barely pink flush. He did not know what to make of Edie's remark that she liked to feel the pearls warm on her neck. But they were hers now, after all. Certainly, they were very pretty and he was glad he had got them for her. Perhaps in the morning he should tell her how strange his insides had been feeling.

On how many more anniversaries would he choose a present for Edie? Some of the gifts on the almanac's list were odd. Sixth anniversary iron, eighth bronze, eleventh steel—what would you give? Fourteen was ivory. Ray thought of that scarlet liquid he had dreamed about. What was that? Was that why he had awakened? Did he feel better? Then there was the Haida display: gold, silver, ivory, slate, and wood. And lace for thirteen. What could a woman give her husband for the thirteenth? Their daughter Evelyn, married a year, bought her husband Japanese desk accessories made of paper—a file holder, a container for pens and paperclips, a waste basket. Ray thought them clever but flimsy. At last he slept, uncomfortably. The other twin bed looked a long way off.

They left New York at last on that humid morning, without Edie's glasses. Edie sat with the other husband, although Ray was not sure how this had happened. Of course the man gave Edie the window seat (not that she would be able to see anything). Ray sat as usual by his window so he could take pictures on the fly, and waited, thoroughly irritated, for the other wife to sit down beside him. But here she was, fluttering, inquiring, was he sure he wouldn't mind, the Florida lady two rows up had a something Ray didn't catch and she would like so much to see it, and so? Gratefully he set his photo bag on the vacant seat and began to lay out his equipment, to look at the diminishing metropolis, to change and change his lenses, filters, settings.

The photo bag—Edie's anniversary present to him—was a great convenience. He took it with him every time he left the bus, ready for canyon, statue, plaque, park, falls, butte, peak, garden, cairn. She could hardly have given him pearls, he supposed. That was the trouble with some of these customs; they only went one way. Perhaps tonight he would tell her that his insides did not feel right. Whatever that dream of scarlet water was, he did not want to dream it again. The blighted suburbs were thinning out.

Edie and the other husband were getting along, it seemed. Ray heard continual low talk, Edie's laugh, more talk. He had not observed any wit in the other husband. Coming up now was a final sharp outline of cityscape, towers flat against sky—he could see the composition precisely. Deftly he swivelled and squinted, and felt his heartbeats. The light was perfect. Click.

He had caught it. Ray felt no pain until he set down the camera, which had pressed against his glasses and driven them into his flesh. His eyes watered in response. He turned smiling to tell her. The unease within came again.

He waited till the dinner stop, but telling Edie in the fluorescent light of the chain restaurant did not feel right. By now, he and Edie and all the others on their tour were thoroughly sick of the Travellers' Rests. Nothing in the fake hard-to-read script on the giant menus looked appetizing any more, and many people on the tour, frugal for decades, were upset by the waste of food. Elderly stomachs faltered before those giant portions. The Travellers' Rest management did not keep a close enough eye on the profit margin, Ray concluded, and thought of the water conserved in those Indian baskets, of the daylight contained in that box.

Leaving the table where Edie and the other husband and the other wife still sat, Ray went to the washroom. He did not like the one on the bus. Its claustrophobic space was too near the other passengers, and Ray now thought that one day something awful might come out of him. He wanted to be alone then. He would not be able to resist bending over to look. His glasses would tip off and leave him right up against a huge flowering oval of watery scarlet brilliance with a dreadful smell. He would jerk up his head and hand and grasp the flush, but that colour and shape would not disappear. As he sat on the toilet in the Travellers' Rest, Ray realized that this daydream felt familiar.

When he got back to Edie at the table (he was still trembling a little), the discussion about the outsize servings of food was culminating. "It's not right," said the other wife, articulating the views of many, "not when there are hungry children in the United States. And Canada," she added, having recently become cognizant of that country.

This statement refreshed the connection between herself and Edie, and—though Ray did not understand why, and said so to Edie in the elevator—after dinner, when the tour had settled in with relief for a not-on-the-road night, Ray and Edie played Scrabble in their room with the other husband and the other wife. Ray's tolerance for this game was low, but the other husband was not a bridge player and Ray estimated that the chattering wife would be useless even for canasta or hearts. And Edie loved Scrabble; Ray watched her fumbling eagerly in her suitcase for the travel-sized game kit.

Ray drew first turn and spelled SELECT, to much praise. The other wife exclaimed several times that if he could only have used his F as well he would have scored fifty extra points. The other husband was quick to follow with CRUX, an over-hasty use of a valuable consonant. The other wife dithered. Then she made TOOT, incredibly, not OX and thirteen more points.

Ray knew Edie would play promptly and acceptably. Her face, looking down at the board, seemed different—of course, no glasses. Her eyelids were full, smooth, white. Ray thought of the Indian eyes, of touching. When had he last wanted to touch Edie? PORTAL, she spelled, and smiled at him, her lashes curling up at the corners of her eyes. To encourage quick play, Ray spelled SHAPE directly. Too late he saw the greater yield of HEAPS.

"Your eyes look just perfect with that dress, dear," said the other wife, "don't they honey?" Honey looked up, first irritated, then admiring. Ray saw his wife. The living and the textile blues intensified each other. Edie's hair glinted in the lamplight. The pearls looked warm, like her cheeks. Perhaps she was tiring? Ray won by more than eighty points. The other wife did not even make one hundred. Edie was next to Ray.

Later, standing in her nightgown, Edie combed her hair before the dresser. The raised moving arm attracted Ray. He found that he was putting his arms around his wife and stroking her pearls and her warm skin and the silky fabric over her breasts. Her astonished face in the mirror smiled at him. Closing his eyes, Ray felt her turn round to face him. Her cheek was firm on his. She was fragrant. Her soft fingers took off his glasses, stroked his skin where the wire and glass and plastic had scored it.

They got themselves across the room and into the big bed. Ray was surprised to find Edie wet; years ago there had been problems with dryness. To be in Edie made Ray deeply happy. They lay as one, moving gently and kissing. Ray realized after a time that no more would happen for him. To make love was so sweet that this almost did not matter. Eventually he lay beside Edie, holding her and stroking her back and sides. She did the same to him. Then he was surprised again, for she took his hand down her body. He touched her only briefly before hearing her small sigh.

Envious, happy, Ray watched his wife go to sleep in his arms. He thought of the Haida. How did they decide whether to use gold, silver, ivory, slate, or wood? Perhaps the dreams said. Perhaps some materials were sacred. Gold had a special value everywhere, he thought. But slate, wood: what did they mean? Those objects must have taken hours mounting to months, years, to complete; Ray knew workmanship when he saw it. What they did with some of those things he could not imagine, but they were definitely well made. Yes. They were beautiful.

You had to look carefully now to find well made goods. Finally he had discovered Edie's necklace at Birks, an old well-established firm. Wonderful, to have seen the same jewels in that French painting a thousand miles away! He would say so to Edie next day, put one of those postcards she'd bought in the album. Beautiful. That brave Frenchman had set out to paint pearls, to use sticky thick dull paste to make them glow in his portrait. At least that artist had seen pearls, though, held them in his hand; the Indians apparently worked from visions. Ray supposed they had made their works for—centuries, would it be? And had travelled the continent barefoot, or lightly shod. Now the buses went all over. Ivory—he puzzled a while. No elephants lived in North America. Thinking it through, he came to walruses.

Ray slept in Edie's arms, untroubled for that one night by dreams.

A Life

She was born in 1954 in a little town in the Fraser Valley of British Columbia. This is dairy country, and when the dairy companies advertise there is no need for camera trickery here. Focus and shoot: an expanse of brilliant silk, so green you cannot think greener, on which stand the Holsteins all paint-box black and white, the tawny Jerseys and the russet Shorthorns. South, where the land relaxes downward into the trees, a blue haze signifies the river. To the north rise the mountains, scissoring the sky. The sun shines, of course, and of course the town, a misshapen nasty smear, does not appear in the photograph.

Of the four children she was the youngest, and the only girl. She resembled her handsome father, who was Dutch. He had come destitute to Canada in 1946, and his rapid English was still haunted by Europe. His eyes were a strong blue, his hair light. A local travel agency had once used a picture of him, amid tulip cut-outs, as a poster. He ran a hardware and farm-implement store; soon he would own it. The boys all took after their plain mother, who was Canadian born of Scottish descent, a warm serviceable woman from the Ottawa Valley. She was wife, and mother to the three hard-driving planful boys and the pretty girl. Inevitably, Wilhelmina

Elizabeth was dressed in frills, her blonde curls were artfully arranged even when there were hardly enough of them to take the comb, and reams of photographs went by jet to Arnprior and Amsterdam.

When she began elementary school, the parents learned that Wilhelmina was too hard for Canadians to say and spell. The child's name became Willa. Mina would have been easier to her father's tongue, but it too sounded funny in Canada, and Elizabeth was more of a tribute than a name intended for personal use—so, Willa. He thought it perfect, so gentle, so pretty. Willa did not do as well in school as her brothers, but no one had expected otherwise, so she had none of the frightening father-interviews endured by the boys when their math or science marks weren't up to par. Patiently, Mr. Hofstra helped Willa with her arithmetic, and stroked her hair when she passed.

Willa's teachers all invariably loved her, and said so to the grateful parents. *Adaptable* and *Fits in well* recurred on report cards in the early sixties. In spite of, because of, her beauty, other children seemed to like her quite well. Her friends were neither as numerous or as loud as those of her brothers—the boys piled hockey gear in the hall, and fought bellowing over car and train games (war games were not allowed) on the rec room floor—but a sharp-faced Shirley-Anne and a stolid Rosalie "came over" from doll-and-cookie time in Grade One till the final semesters of high school. Willa went to all possible birthday parties, got all possible Valentines, and was for years cast as Mary in the Sunday School's Nativity Play. There was even a kind of community pride in the child's beauty. On November Saturdays when Willa went with her father to see the boys play hockey, friends would clamber up the bleachers to say, "Looking forward to seeing you in that lovely blue robe again, Willa!" Her father would hold her hand tightly, and tremble.

Once in high school, Willa spent Saturday mornings with her mother in the kitchen; of course she had always helped with the cooking, but now her serious training began. Mrs. Hofstra had come to marriage with a solid rural Ontario repertoire of roasts, stews, breads, pies, and pickles, and over the years had thoroughly enjoyed learning European approaches to fish, organ meats, rye flours, ground nuts, and bitter chocolate. She relished the use of herbs and spices. Now she sought to pass on what she knew to her daughter. She could not. Willa could follow a recipe, do what her mother told her, but of the crucial ability to survey the contents of a refrigerator or to assess the character of a cut of meat and thence to deduce a menu or a dish, there was no sign. Perhaps this skill would come in time? but Mrs. Hofstra could not remember being without it. She could not put a name to her worry. A report card arrived. *Friendly* yes, *Completes her assignments* yes, and then *Willa shows little initiative.* The father snorted. "There is no trouble here. See, she has passed everything. She should not be like that crazy Shirley-Anne, always arguing, a new crazy idea every week, you do not want that? She is fine, our beautiful girl."

Not quite convinced, the mother sought to discuss the report card with Willa. Her daughter said, without expression, "I don't think Miss Ridley likes me much, Mum." Well. Mrs. Hofstra still found it hard to believed that Willa had emerged from her own thickwaisted unremarkable body; still, on her own birthdays, she knelt to thank her God for giving her such a husband. In that way Willa would have no trouble, no weeping in the night. Well. It would be all right.

Indeed, Willa was sought after. There were rules, of course, much stricter than those for the boys had been; Willa never argued with them, nor with the requirement that the boy must come into the house and meet the parents properly before he drove Willa away to the dance or movie. So the phone rang and rang, and out Willa went. By the end of Grade Ten she had been taken out by more boys than her mother had to the point of her marriage at twenty-three. The only guidance on sex that Willa received was a book placed on her bedside table on her twelfth birthday. She did not ask any questions about it. Each of her parents, without discussing the matter with the other, was quite sure that Willa did not need to be told what not to do with boys.

The bright sleek fashions of the late sixties suited Willa. She was meticulous in her grooming, her choice of jewellery and accessories. She and Rosalie spent afternoons looking through fashion magazines, choosing, analysing, comparing. When Willa turned sixteen her parents gave her a sewing machine, which delighted her as much as had the dollhouse on her sixth. She began searching in pattern books for her graduation outfit. "And soon after that you'll be making another white dress, eh Willa?" asked her father fondly. Willa smiled her rare smile. "In a hurry to give me away, are you Dad?"

No no no, he was not. He could not in fact imagine doing so. Where was the man who would be good enough? He thought about the files of boys whose hands he had shaken in his own living-room. Why did so many boys call? No, that was not the right question, of course it was because she was so pretty. Rather—why did they not call for a second date? Hardly ever did a boy take Willa out more than twice. No signs of a steady. Just as well, probably; there was Shirley-Anne with her biker, all jeans and eyeshadow and tobacco breath, he did not like to have her in the house really, and there was Rosalie, swaying from one hopeless crush to another with months of wailing in between. Well. Some day he would walk with his daughter down the aisle of the new stucco church, that was certain. He wondered if her heart had yet been touched, and then felt red warmth coming up his throat. Did those boys not come back because they had so soon got what they wanted from his Willa? Something told him *No*. The red receded. He did not know how to speak his thoughts to his wife.

In the autumn of Willa's last year in high school the white dress lay basted in its tissue, and eight boys already had asked her to the grad dance. At this time the youngest Hofstra brother, Pete (Pieter on his birth certificate), was in his second year of engineering at UBC, following the older boys who were now at work in the Alberta oil-fields. Pete's girlfriend Helen conceived a child. When the father-son interview took place in the Hofstra living-room, Willa was in the kitchen with her mother, helping to make Christmas cakes. Mr. Hofstra's accent was stronger than in years and the English syntax fought him, but the words still fell like boulders: seduce, sin, betray, ruin, lust, atone. Inevitably, he concluded by asking "How could you do this to your mother?" Silence. Mrs. Hofstra began to cry. She gripped the edge of the kitchen counter and her tears fell on to the pile of sultanas and grated lemon rind. Willa stirred methodically. When her mother was calm again, Willa said, "It was her fault, Mum. She shouldn't have let him." Mrs. Hofstra looked blearily at her daughter. She felt frightened. She felt ugly.

Early in the New Year, Willa's parents observed that Rosalie and Shirley-Anne were not coming over to the house, and that one particular young man had begun to date Willa regularly. This one's name was Bud. Mr. Hofstra did not like that. "He has a real name, surely?" His nickname was the only thing, however, that could possibly be held against him. He was twenty-four; that was a nice age difference. He was in law school. His father was one of the town's noted lawyers, the families went to the same church, and he was as good-looking in a smooth dark way as Willa was in her blondeness. Balm flowed over the wounds Pete had inflicted. (Mrs. Hofstra was knitting energetically for the coming grandchild, but did not take her work with her when visiting friends.) The Hofstras settled themselves to watch and wait as Willa and Bud moved through the Valentines' Dance and the school's Easter Prom and the UBC Spring Fling. Mrs. Hofstra made herself not ask her daughter how she had extricated herself from her original date for the grad dance, and the night she saw Willa go down the sidewalk in her radiant dress to Bud's new Mustang was one of the happiest of her adult life. The young couple announced a week later that they would marry in the following spring.

Now it would not do for Willa to be sitting at home all the time, and so she worked mornings in one of her father's stores, cashiering. For a while Mr. Hofstra teased her about her mistakes. "You have something nicer to think about than ringing up the sales tax every time, I know that, Willa. But for now you must remember, my dear." Later he became impatient, and later still he snapped at her, the first time ever. Willa did not cry, or argue. It was soon understood that completing her trousseau and shopping for furniture with her mother occupied so much of her time that she could not longer take the mornings "off." Mrs. Hofstra had her own problems with Willa. The prospective bride could show her mother exactly what she wanted on the pages of magazines: linens, silver, crystal, flowers, chairs, bridesmaids' gowns. But no, she did not want the old Pembroke table shipped out from Ontario when Granny died, and no, she did not want the heavy cream lace tablecloth which had spent the war years buried underneath an espaliered peach tree in Oma's garden. No. These and similar items would not fit into Willa's decor, Willa's colour-scheme. "But Willa, don't you want . . . ?" asked Mrs. Hofstra, and could not think how to finish. She wrote cheques on the special and generous account which Mr. Hofstra had set up.

When Willa's father paid the wedding photographer, the man said, "It's been a pleasure, sir," and for once meant it. It would be hard to imagine a more beautiful series of wedding pictures than those recording that June day of 1973 when Willa became Mrs. Brian Conrad. When her veil was raised, Willa tilted her head so as to receive Bud's kiss on her cheek. Many guests found this *pudeur* charming. Mrs. Hofstra had a very different memory of her own wedding, but the compliments paid and the warm wishes expressed on the receiving line would have gladdened any parent. Mrs. Hofstra could feel her husband's hand trembling in hers. By the end of the reception the groom had taken rather more champagne than he should, and had also tried to feel up both the bridesmaids; Shirley-Anne and Rosalie only told each other.

One day in early December of that year, Mr. and Mrs. Hofstra were picking up their car after its regular maintenance and encountered their son-in-law. The transmission on the Mustang had gone. There never seemed to be a great deal to say to Bud, but Mrs. Hofstra was smiling warmly and her husband was beginning to speak jovially about Christmas plans when the young man interrupted. "Didja know Wil's pregnant?"

Mrs. Hofstra was the more upset. Mr. Hofstra was mostly concerned about how the young family would manage financially—Bud was in his articling year. The fathers met. Bud's notions of a high-powered Vancouver career were set aside; he would join his father's firm in the town. Mr. Hofstra was then free to experience unalloyed pride in legitimate grand-fatherhood. Pete and Helen's little son was bittersweetness for him, but here now could be plain joy. His wife could not feel with him. At first, she was simply hurt because Willa had not told her. This pain was severe. Then Willa arrived for family Christmas dinner wearing a tight crimson dress and a tighter girdle. The mother's gravy had lumps in it. Willa ate little, Bud was loud, and the elder Conrads were not talkative people.

The baby was due in May, and from January on Willa scarcely left her home. Her mother visited her daily. Willa would not wear the charming maternity outfits which Mrs. Hofstra and Mrs. Conrad gave her, would not look at the catalogues from Mothercare. She stayed all day in her honeymoon gowns, passing hours at her dressing table with her hair and makeup. Although she chatted at length with Shirley-Anne and Rosalie when they phoned, she did not ask them over. Mrs. Hofstra watched TV, knitted, crocheted, cleaned, cleaned again. Once weekly, the parents came formally to dinner with their daughter and son-in-law. Willa did not really cook, but served the most expensive convenience foods available. At first Mr. Hofstra was amused, as he had been at Willa's spindly furniture and at the white-shag carpet in her bathroom. Later he complained of not feeling fed, and ate slabs of cheese and ham and honeycake when he got home.

At Easter, settling his daughter in her chair at the loaded Hofstra table, the father said teasingly, "Nothing is from a package here, eh Willa? Soon you'll be able to cook like this again." Willa did not respond. She refused dessert. She refused to be in the family pictures after lunch, in spite of Bud's maudlin pleading: "Aw Wil? C'mon, Wil." The Hofstras met in the kitchen and saw each other's distress. Then they went out again and did their best with the Conrads. Pete and Helen and the little one arrived after lunch, and that helped.

Bud phoned, drunk, at one o'clock of a May morning to tell the Hofstras they had a granddaughter. Mr. Hofstra wept, and his wife held him. She was not surprised next afternoon in the hospital when Willa would not talk to her about the birth, for both grandfathers as well as Bud were at the bedside. Willa wore lacy white. Her fatigue made her look even younger than she was. After three more days, however, Mrs. Hofstra understood that Willa was not going to talk about her labour at all. She talked about the starchy hospital food, and the exercises she must do to flatten her stomach, and—briefly—about the inadequacy of her milk supply and the excellence of formula. Mrs. Hofstra thought, felt, back to the four occasions on which she had entered the exhilarating field of labour. Each was distinct in her body's memory.

Small at birth, the child Kimberley gained weight slowly and cried a great deal. She was said to have colic. She was dark, like her father, and fine-featured, with a neat piquancy that was the reverse of the fat-faced Gerber baby look. "A European girl, this one," said Mr. Hofstra, immensely pleased. The christening photographs were exquisite. Willa was as slender as ever, and the baby's lace flowed gracefully down her deep blue dress.

Kimberley was eight months old when, one afternoon, the Hofstras stopped off at Willa's to deliver some beef for her freezer. There was no answer to their knock, but Willa must be home because they could hear Kimberley screaming. "Hello! Hello!" and cheerfully they went in. No Willa anywhere. The baby's room stank of urine and feces and vomit. Baby clothes, beautifully knitted and embroidered, lay in filthy bloodspotted heaps on the floor. With trembling hands, the grandfather heated a bottle according to his wife's frantic instructions, and returned with it to Kimberley's room—the window now stood open to the fresh air over the valley fields—to find Mrs. Hofstra in tears, holding the naked shrieking infant whose lower parts were raw and whose limbs were ringed with bruises.

They tried to talk to Bud. No, he didn't know Wil was doing stuff like this. Yes, he'd seen that she wasn't real involved with Kim, but when he was around she always got fed and changed, as far as he knew. He wasn't around much though, his father was making him work his—work very hard. Mr. and Mrs. Hofstra tried to tell Bud what it had been like when Willa finally came home (from where?). Without interest, she looked at the baby's polished room, the piles of washed and folded small garments, the thick cornstarch paste Mrs. Hofstra had applied to Kimberley's buttocks and vulva. Mr. Hofstra had gone out to buy rusks for the baby; Willa held them in her hands while her parents spoke to her with urgent tenderness. The Hofstras felt their words fall unheard into nothing. Frightened, they left. "We are frightened, Bud," they said. "We don't understand." He listened. At the end, he said, "She's having another, you know."

In the following months, Mrs. Hofstra left her own house each weekday morning right after an early breakfast, and went to Willa's. She returned after Bud had got home from work. If he was needed at his father's law office in the evenings, Mr. Hofstra went over to his daughter's. Quite often, he had to stay overnight there.

Sometimes Willa sat in her old way looking into the mirror, and changed from gown to gown until the bed was heaped with discarded costumes. Mostly she sat in the livingroom or lay on the couch in the den, staring at whatever happened to be in front of her. Her mother would steer Willa to a chair near the TV, so at least she would look as though she were seeing something. Meanwhile, Mrs. Hofstra cared for Kimberley.

Once she asked Shirley-Anne and Rosalie to visit, saying with a stiff throat, "Willa's not too well. Maybe you'd come cheer her up a bit, surprise her?" For half an hour Willa laughed and talked, as the girls recalled Miss Ridley's awful sweaters and the prom night of their junior year. The visitors praised Mrs. Hofstra's coffeecake. Willa even ate a cookie. But when Rosalie mentioned her accounting job at the dairy and Shirley-Anne talked about the commercial art course she was taking, Willa's face went null. She turned on the TV abruptly. Red with embarrassment, Mrs. Hofstra asked the visitors to come see Kimberley, just then waking from her nap. Willa did not accompany them. Her friends left, and did not return.

Willa's son was born in the dry of early September, when hollow grass whispered under the brush of the wind. This time, the Hofstras were notified by the hospital staff. Bud was out somewhere drunk, and had been so for a week, off and on. Mrs. Conrad had come to stay at the house, and had driven Willa to the hospital when her labour began. The new grandchild was Brian Junior, to be called Bri, and was all the grandparents could wish: a big blond boy, vigorous and assertive. Looking at the wriggling limbs, the Hofstras and the Conrads felt amazed that such boisterous vitality could emerge from Willa's delicate languor.

The elder Conrads escorted their grandson and Willa home from the hospital. Small Kimberley was to stay with the Hofstras "until Willa got on her feet." Alone, Mrs. Hofstra went to see her daughter at home with her new baby, and came back to blubber in relief on Mr. Hofstra's chest. "It's all right. It's going to be all right this time." Willa held the baby close, she smiled and cooed and made kissing noises, she talked about his weight and his skin and his hair and his toenails. "She wouldn't even let me hold him!"

Willa would not let anyone hold him. Waking, Bri lay diagonally like an Order across his mother's torso, or rested on the shelf of her hip; sleeping, he lay with her on a cot set up in his room. When he napped, visitors had to be silent. Frequently Willa called the doctor about Bri, and the medicine cabinet was full of pastes, creams, washes. The baby's formula and then his pablum and mashed banana were prepared as if for a patient in intensive care. Very soon Bri became plump, then fat. In his christening photograph, he lay alone on cushions frothed with lace, gazing up with eyes like blue marbles in lard.

Each afternoon now, Mr. Hofstra left one or other of his stores a little early. His businesses went well, better every year, it seemed he could not make a mistake there if he tried, and so it was nice to feel a little freer now, with the grandchildren to spend time with. When he got home, he would arrange Kimberley in her stroller with her bright crocheted poncho over her, and wheel her through the chilly streets for a visit to the house where the child's mother and father and brother lived. These trips gave Mr. Hofstra great pleasure. The small bundled creature chortled and kicked in her stroller, and smiled when he pointed out dogs, rosebuds, lawnmowers. She gestured and exclaimed; she liked birds especially. Certain streets pleased her more than others, so she chose which way they should go. She was talking now. He shared her delight in words. The Hofstra grandparents were Gummy and Gamma, and they all three laughed—but day after day after day went by, Bri was almost four months old, and still Willa did not say, "It's time Kim came home."

Finally, Mrs. Hofstra said to Mr. Hofstra: "Well then, you say it to her."

He found this act most difficult. At last he made the words come out, while Willa was bathing Bri. Had she actually heard him? She made no objection, at least. On a certain Tuesday, therefore, with great and loving ceremony provided by the Hofstras, Kimberley returned.

At noon on the Wednesday—a day of icy-grey rain, in January—Mr. Hofstra drove by Willa's on his way home for lunch. He had a packet of chocolate, shaped like a duck, for Kimberley. Outside the house was a police car, its bewildering lights flashing blue-red, blue-red. A cop held Kimberley, who wore nothing, was cold soaking wet and muddy, and had a vicious black eye. Several neighbours stood about. A woman identified herself as a social worker to Mr. Hofstra. Humiliation fired his entire body. When Kimberley saw her grandfather, she stretched out her naked self to him imploringly, and screamed. The cop handed her over. The child clung to Mr. Hofstra so hard she drew blood at the back of his neck. Holding her, he looked up at the drawn curtains of his daughter's home.

A month or so later, Mrs. Hofstra was at Willa's house, with Kimberley—accompanied visits of a few hours were all right—

and they were baking Valentine cookies. The little girl messed happily with flour and an extra rolling-pin, and made her own shapes with the bits of dough her grandmother gave her. They laughed together. Bri lay sluggish in his basket. When he started to whimper, Mrs. Hofstra went to rouse Willa from her long afternoon sleep. The thin young woman lay on her side. The bodice of her grubby pink nightgown had fallen forward to expose her left breast. The smooth skin was dimpled, as though a mouth were forming in the flesh.

Even before Kimberley and her grandmother could ice and serve the Valentine cookies, Willa had no breasts. The Hofstras and the Conrads, Rosalie and Shirley-Anne gathered at the hospital. They tried not to look at the non-shape under the skimpy hospital gown, and also tried not to look into Willa's eyes, because she hardly ever blinked and the resultant stare was upsetting. The visitors talked as much as they could, to cover up Willa's complete silence and the fact that Bud wasn't there. He hadn't appeared since the day of the x-rays. Sometimes he phoned his mother or mother-in-law from pay phones, mumbled and swore. The Conrads took Bri.

The disease metastasized in Willa like fire consuming a nylon stocking. A few days before the terminal coma, her voice was heard again, at an amazing volume. "Does she hear herself, I wonder?" Mr. Hofstra said aloud, just to hear a voice against the sound, as he sat by his daughter's side. Occasionally she lay quiet. Then he patted her fingerbones, and said, "Soon. Soon, I promise you, Wilhelmina."

The Skein

One

Your first dream is The Case of the Baby with the Cracked Skull.

You are in a bar or lounge, dark, crowded, underground, that opens off a passageway under a downtown hotel. The carpeting is midnight blue.

The people you are with are not with you. You are walking towards them, past tables at which drinkers sit, past the bar with the serried glasses and the spigots for the liquor. Talk and laughter are all around in the dark.

You carry a baby, not your baby, whose head rests on your left arm. The mother has asked you to take care of the baby for a while. Maybe she is just in the washroom or getting a Coke, but you feel she is doing something more important, like making a speech or having a crucial conversation.

As you walk, slowly, you look down at this baby. You don't like the look of it—small, emaciated, with a large head, dark-skinned, like the starving Ethiopian children. That blanket wrapped round the baby used to lie on your brother's bed at the summer cottage. A soft old cosy thing of royal blue flannel with olive greyhounds running by the hem, it folds round the baby to make a mummy-shape.

You become aware of dampness on your left arm. To inspect, you gently turn the child's head to one side.

The skull is multiply cracked. The child's hair is dark, nappy, and there is the head-bone. Blood shimmers through, red fluid bubbling through a crazed boiling egg.

All your flesh shivers in fear.

If you wrap the baby's head carefully, perhaps the mother will not notice when you give the baby back.

Perhaps you yourself dropped this baby? Perhaps you did. You don't remember the drop. But you know it fell. You know it fell on this very carpet, blue that masks a hard hard floor; you can feel the hardness through stockings and shoes and carpet and underlay. Yes, this baby fell. You hear the soft awful sound of the head hitting.

You waken from this dream.

In the thin dark, the curtains and the rug are porous membranes; the air is grey *pointilliste* gas, hanging in sheets.

You cry out.

You cry, loudly. No one is there.

The quilt is stuffy and damp, your back cold, the sheets rumpled and hurtful.

Quickly you get up. You walk.

You walk naked through the rooms, repeatedly, quickly, then more slowly.

You walk, sensing the bulk of the huge night-time furniture, the unfamiliar objects on the bookcase, the sill. The startled cat on the sofa leaps away from you. You walk.

Your breasts are cold. You walk.

By the sink stands a partial glass of flat cola. Why is there nothing to do but to drink, and go back to bed? Your skin shudders. Nothing. Cold against your inner surfaces, the liquid trickles down inside your body.

Sleep—another room to run to.

This sleep you enter now, after your awful dream, is a heavy blotter. Dehydrated, the contents of your skull split multiply. The fissures design a crazy paving, an ad for moisturizer, a petrified Gobi.

The day, the day, when will it come? You want the day so badly. You want to know that there are three, four, seven hours between you and that dreadful dream. You want the day, not what will be in it or what you will do in it, but just the day itself to get to you, to your part of the world.

The daylight does come, eventually. You are very tired, and wish you could sleep and sleep. But the day has come. The bed is hateful, the room. You go into the day.

Lubricant of one day.
Another day.
Another day.
Passive, passing.
A day, another day.

Gradually, the emollients are absorbed. The tissue is stiff, but not rigid, with fear and pain.

You find the recipe for poppyseed cake.

Nice. Good. That will be nice. Sit in the garden, eat a summer cake, drink a pale cool drink.

You pour two cups of poppyseeds into the old blue mixing bowl.

You pour spheres, thousands of tiny spheres, each smaller and less brilliant than a blackberry nodule, tiny ballbearings, shining, shining like pewter; you pour a dense black-blue pouring down to form a blunt cone of globes. Each swells with a scarlet flower on a slender hairy stem of celadon. Inside each is rumoured to be sleep.

The seeds, the pouring, the summer thoughts are lubricant.

You begin to think you can move towards the hard lumps of pain thrown up by the dream.

Can you touch one?

Try.

Try touching the thought that you thought of not telling the mother.

You thought of lying to her.

You are a liar. You are a liar. A liar. A liar, and there is no truth in you.

Your resistance must still be low, for the pain flashes and the drycaked gobbets all split their sides and blood runs out and the judge arrives, right away, right, even while you're stuttering and sputtering. He sweeps a big fleshy wing across the table where you've offered up your stupid little stammerings and *Peh!* They're gone. The wood is bare. You are a liar. His wings are dark red, heavily muscled.

You have lied. Memories trip over each other to testify, like witnesses at the Moscow Trials (there was truth there, too). Lies rush out from elementary school, high school, family school, graduate school, marriage school. Hateful words and phrases live in remembered speech; there are worse silences, dead air, cowardly.

The worst are the lies you still do not understand why you told. Most of these are from the marriage, are full of corruption, like boils—no, like tumours, blind growths unwilling to shape an orifice, determined to eat from within.

Distress. Throughout the body, distress, dis-ease. Like bad flu, the disorder of the dream, or its frightful order, weighs down your flesh so that your body grows heavy. Your mind and emotions sink into thickness. Dulled, slowed, you feel only this suffusing malaise. The person is going to come to a stop.

The cat's sweet fur brushes your hand. Automatically you repeat the stroke, repeat. Her eyes are gingery green, her nose cold as a kiss.

You're not strong enough yet.

You need days more.

You need days scattered with the table spices of domestic life: the smooth cut of a letter-opener as it moves under beloved handwriting, the line and colour of pears in a pieplate, the child's skates that still fit this year, good, the paperboy serious on the porch in the rain. You need days in which first minutes, then half-hours, then hours go by when the screen of consciousness is empty of the dream; your mind minds, your feelings feel, but the oozing skull and the shudder of fear and the thud of the dropping baby are not there.

Days, days more to recover.

At work you start, slowly, to be more than an automaton. Meetings occur at which you are present in more than name. Here. You are there. You can even do what you are good at, in meetings: hear the common note in the words of many, sound it so they can hear too. You can put it in writing. You write it down.

To the student with the dangling modifier, you reveal the healing magic. You see the smile of understanding, know the sentence is forever whole. Feeling useful is now possible.

Even crossing the border to sleep is not hard any more. There you are no citizen, however. You wake at three almost nightly, deported, holding no other papers (they have all been destroyed). More than an hour must go by, somewhere, before you re-enter—sometimes two hours, three. You try all the tricks of hot milk and reading and a low radio like an overheard conversation among bores. Sometimes one or another influences the guards, and you go back, to sleep. You dream no dreams, but every time you sleep, you remember that tonight may end that.

Days, nights, days.

Times come now when your flesh seems smoothly fitted to your bones, not as though dragging down their surfaces. The tissue itself feels less dense. The weighted wires under the skin of your face are pliant again.

You are ready for another attempt.

Better. Better, this time, among the dry gobbets, the huge caked chunks in that field inside your head. Yes, a short rush of pain meets your touch of the memory, but it's like opening a jar of solvent, javex, pickles: after the burst, calm.

Slowly you begin to walk over the petrified rubble.

You look round boulders, shoulder-high.

The river of blood sings underneath, yes, but no springs, no fountains bubble up; you are still far from the headwaters. When you pick up a lump and brush off the dried clay and sand, the light spray of particles disperses rapidly. Soundless, the tiny things fall.

What is this you are holding? This is the time—well, it is one of many, but you know which one—that you did not tell him of your angry hurt. Specifically, you did not tell him of your hurt anger at his happy encouragement of you to "get as much work as possible" in the outreach teaching centre. This occurred when there was a newborn baby and he was determinedly unemployed, dedicated to important unpaid political work, spending long hours on the phone or at meetings, baby on his shoulder or in his lap.

You turn the gobbet over. Yes, there is more to this one. You kept all the anger and the pain within. Within, they acted according to that inexorable law you must repeatedly relearn: pain unspoken accumulates intensity. (How does that happen, in the closed head? Do the hurt and rage ferment like wine, hang like meat?)

In the unspeaking container, those feelings were preserved in fullness to an early morning, years later, when you snatched them from storage and threw them as hard as you could. Thrown, they did heavy damage. (Still they weight the shelf of memory, though they are not so substantial now. They radiate a less virulent aura. Why do some pains stay, jagged ghosts, while others dissipate? Some only pretend to go; years later, a phrase or a look or the colour of a woollen sleeve will dump you up to your neck in the battery acid of remembered misery.)

You rotate the gobbet of dried pain in your palms.

What is the link between these: your memory of not telling and your dream of a thought of not telling?

You put the lump down, watch puffs of pale dust blow up, subside.

Within you is a tremble and a shivering, but not disaster. You can go on doing this, examining, considering. You can even let controlled quantities of feeling occur.

Why does the dream include the blanket from your brother's bed at the cottage? That baby, whoever it may be, is wrapped in safety and love.

Maybe you are the ugly baby. You have dropped yourself, out of neglect. You have been injured but will not tell yourself so. You will not let the word come through the flesh, but here it is, trickling over your arm, so the loveblanket is red with that fatal damp. Why will you not tell yourself? Why did you not tell him? What were, are, you frightened of?

Here is the judge again, but this time you are not quite overwhelmed. You can even look briefly into his eyes.

"Why were you underground?" he asks in that harsh voice. His wings throb as the red feathers ruffle into their ranks.

Your mind perks up with the obvious answers, a good little girl at school: I was going down into myself; I was entering parts of myself I usually keep underneath and in the dark.

"Yes yes, but why a hotel?" The judge's emphasis tells of his irritation at your superficiality.

"I was journeying," you say. The disapproving atmosphere, like an excess of gravity, weighs your words towards the floor. The judge's huge scarlet face makes a *moue*, grotesque in that mass of skin. His eyes dilate.

"Why didn't you know where she was? Getting a cheap drink, making a speech—bosh. They're different, can't you see that? Think."

The judge never responds to what you have said, only to what you have failed to say. Guilt is rising in you like dirty water in a glass.

When your daughters were little, you left them in hastily-assembled conference daycares while you attended sessions, made speeches. You left them. You dropped them off. So the child with the cracked skull is your daughter or daughters, and you will not admit to yourself what you have done.

Oh brother. Even with the judge's glare full on your face and sweat running over your skin like fluid out of salted eggplant, a part of you says contemptuously *Oh brother.*

The glad eye of intellect observes how right it feels to feel wrong! to feel observed as wrong! The feeling calls with the powerful voice of the known, of home, your mother yodelling over the lake in summer when the time came to turn the canoe towards the bay and dinner. When you feel most wrong, you feel most yourself. Wrongness moves living and heavy through your blood and through the chambers of your brain. You feel a thickening now, as if the pores in your bones were filling in with lead . . . . *No.* You pull back.

You can, now, pull back. That ability distinguishes this from the earlier phases of the recovery from the dream. You pull back. You don't feel well, but you have not succumbed.

You look at the ingredients in the recipe: poppyseeds, sugar, flour, baking powder, oil, eggs, milk, vanilla, orange zest, bananas.

First comes the blue-blackness of the poppyseed cone, and last come the bananas, curved like the moon and as yellow, spotted like the tongue of the tigerlily, smooth and solid and self-contained as snakes. Their colour and radiance are benevolent; their parenthetical arches have a dancer's grace. You remember the first-born eating her first solid food. A tiny plop of almost-liquid banana peaks on the tip of the advancing spoon—and her astonished face as the yellow meets her tastebuds! You feel better already.

That other broken baby, thin and alien, is not yours, remember?

The judge makes his guttural cawing sound. Like taffeta in a winter wind, his wings rustle. "That's all very well," he utters, "all very well for you to say."

You are not yet well. You are only better.

Two

A river: the streaming, the meandering, the rushing, the double motion created by the wind against the current against the wind—all form a flowing process targeted to the sea. She is the swimmer.

In her case, case study, case history, in the case of her, there occur dreadful sinkholes, sinkrivers, collapses, implosions. Worse than rapids, these cannot be bypassed. There are no portages. She hits the rocks, she strikes rock, her head strikes, is stuck under torrential water and fallen branches. She knows that rivers have been known to vanish, to be swallowed. Meanwhile, her known landscape with the river's run across it is no more. Unfamiliar landforms loom, fanged with torn earth and roots.

To date, she has survived. How? By not breathing. By struggling sightlessly. Life-sustaining techniques of limited value, surely—but she is still here.

(Almost two years after the Case of the Baby with the Cracked Skull, she speculates: Perhaps *she* did not drop the baby? Perhaps the mother gave her the damaged baby, chose her as an appropriate caregiver for an endangered child.)

She is on the Island for the weekend, with her thirteen-year-old daughter Mary; her good friend Hannah; her friend Ruth. They are staying in a small cabin. Also with them is Hannah's baby (although in the waking world Hannah has no baby), who is a few months old and seriously ill.

So there are five, women and girl and sick baby. The clinic is closed, the doctor and nurse off-Island. No ferries sail from any of the Gulf Islands till Monday. The women face their responsibility to keep the baby alive.

Calmly they talk, sitting at the table that overlooks the beach and the grey ocean, drinking coffee, passing the baby around from time to time while they plan babycare shifts so each of them can get some sleep and not leave the baby a moment unattended. If so left, the baby will die, for its nose and throat generate streams of a substance not so much wet as stiff, stuff that comes out like sprayed arcs of hair-lacquer hanging in the air. Constantly the women wipe the baby's nose, open its mouth and wipe the sticky mucus out. More mucus, like web from a dozen spiders' spinnerets, springs out as they work. Their fingers are thick in the baby's tiny mouth, at the nostrils.

While the women attend the baby, Mary the older daughter sits nearby. She is naked and reading. Her entire body is covered with big soft clear blisters. To break them feels to the finger exactly like breaking bubblepack. Their breaking is not painful to Mary; as she reads, she breaks one occasionally herself, absent-mindedly, as one might fiddle with strands of hair or a belt. Hence, the name of this dream: the Case of the Blistered Child.

Her mother knows that Mary is sick, and Mary knows that she is sick, and they both know, in the dream, that her sickness is not as important as the baby's. That Mary experiences discomfort is the worst of her physical state; however, she is miserable to be so disfigured. Her mother knows that. What lovely skin Mary used to have—and the mother wipes away her springing tears because there is a baby to keep alive till Monday.

From this dream the woman goes directly into memory, for this image—the cabin by the water with the little people arranged round the table—takes her right back to when she was eight and had the measles. Lying abed with the winter light striping obliquely through the shutters, she heard her mother and brother talking in the long bare hall outside her room.

"She'll love it," her mother said. "D'you think you can have it ready for Christmas?"

"Sure. Sure I can." Much older than she, he seemed always sure he could. This secret involved hammering.

Recovering, and moving aimlessly about the house—she was not to go back to school until the New Year—the little girl repeatedly came across her mother sewing, by hand. Extraordinary. Not until she had got the dollhouse on Christmas Day and screamed for joy did she think back and see that the things being sewn had been so small. Here they were now, cushions and curtains, bedspreads, tablecloths, napkins even, a blue felt carpet; and here also were tiny oil-paintings, flowers and fruit, on all the walls.

The house was solid, and its size perfect for some little dolls she already had. Her brother had designed the dwelling to fit them, had carved and painted a wooden cat and dog to move in with the family—an English sheepdog, a marmalade tom. All the furniture, square-cut and chunky in a rather Bauhaus style, was also of her brother's making. He had sensibly built the staircase up the outside of the house, instead of taking up all that space inside, so manoeuvering the dolls on their journeys up and downstairs was much easier than in a conventional dollhouse. There was even a bathroom (though it had no toilet). He had contrived, with plastic tubing and a turkey baster, a means of filling the china bathtub and emptying it again.

She could imagine no more wonderful present.

That summer when the dolls and humans all went to the cottage, the dollhouse went too, strapped to the roof of the old Pontiac. For two long green sunny months it stood on attractive lakeshore acreage, well-treed, beautiful sandy beach, sunset view, excellent swimming and fishing (though neither the human nor the doll family ever fished, and the dolls were not swimmers). For those months, the dramas centred on ocean cruises, on journeying with Peary to the Pole, and on the circumnavigation—a wonderful new word learned in school that year—of the globe.

Always after that summer the dollhouse smelled different; even in the city, its wood gave off a watery scent. Crisp sand sparkled in the corners of the rooms.

Thirty-odd years later, this girl, this woman has young daughters of her own.

This woman's old mother says, "Oh, I would love your girls to have a dollhouse!"

The woman's first reaction is enthusiasm—understandable. When the old mother repeats her exclamation, the woman begins to translate.

The mother: Oh, I would love your girls to have a dollhouse! [I wish you led a proper life. I wish you lived in a real house with the bedrooms upstairs, not in an apartment in a housing co-op, whatever that is, with those basement bedrooms and the ground ivy growing over the windows. I wish your girls wore dresses with matching coats and took piano lessons. I wish they played the way you used to, in your attic playroom with the nine dolls and sixteen stuffed animals. I wish you were young again and that I was too. I wish we could sit together and sew little things for your daughters' dollhouse, but you have to work so hard because of that man and you have chosen to live three thousand miles away from me.]

The woman: A dollhouse? That would be nice. [Are you offering to buy the girls a dollhouse? You know I can't buy one and furnish it. You know I barely have enough for our housing charges and food, that the only new clothes we get except underwear are presents from you. Even though you ask in that critical voice why I'm still wearing "that old thing," I know you know why. What I don't understand is the motivation of that query. Perhaps you hope that under your questioning I will break, will boohoo all my unhappiness out on you, and give you authority to take me away from That Man and put me in prison again. The jail of home. Or perhaps you fantasize that the word will make flesh, that by asking why I don't subscribe to *Gourmet* or reupholster the livingroom sofa you will generate stacks of back issues on the coffeetable in front of the new chintz pleats. Well, mother—if you do give them a dollhouse, I hope you don't present it like the crown jewels. You always give with strings attached. And he won't like it, however you do it, because it's you doing it.]

The mother: What do you think? Shall that be my present to them, for Christmas? [I can just see how the girls will look, kneeling by the Christmas tree, leaving the biggest thing till last, wondering and guessing. I won't tell them, of course. They will be happy. They will thank me. They will love me. Their father can't object to that, even he can't. He can't tell a grandmother not to give a dollhouse to her granddaughters. He can't stop me this time. I can tell people, "I'm giving the girls a dollhouse for Christmas. Yes, they haven't got one. I'm giving it." She can take photographs. I'll show people the photographs.]

The woman: Where is my old dollhouse? The one brother made me? [Now that I *would* like. I'd love to have the kids play with my old dollhouse, to tell them about the plays I used to play, to try and remember the names of my dolls, to watch them fill the bathtub. The kids always get a kick out of stuff my brother and I did when we were little. I haven't thought of that dollhouse in years.]

The mother: Oh, in the garage, I suppose, what's left of it. It's all battered about, dear. It wouldn't do. [No. That would make it your present. I want this to be my present. I want them to have new things. I know you buy them clothes at the Salvation Army and awful places like that, so pleased because you got that lovely long frilled dress for a dollar, dreadful. I won't have it. My daughter and my grandchildren should have new things, good things, made just for them. I want to give them a new dollhouse.]

The woman: Oh. [Why do I feel hurt that my old dollhouse is all beat up? Why, when I haven't given it a thought for years? Nothing of mine is good enough, nothing of me. Not good enough, not good enough . . . . The kids would love a dollhouse. She wants to do this, I can tell. Badly. Doing it will give her pleasure. There's not much of that in her life. There's not likely to be much. He won't like it, because it's from her. He'll find some reason to be against it. There'll be trouble. My stomach is knotting up already.] Okay, Mum, go ahead.

The husband: Why did you let her talk you into it? What are we going to do with some damn huge dollhouse? You know how small the girls' rooms are. It's just another way for her to control, for her to tell us how to live. And of course you said *yes*. Stupid bourgeois notion, a dollhouse. [This does not need translation.]

What would have happened if she had said *No, Mum, I don't think so?*

The mother: Oh. Well, dear, if you don't want my present . . . . [Pain, pain, my baby that I longed for is saying no to me. She doesn't want what I offer. I can never get it right, never see what it is she really wants. She won't tell me. I don't know her. But this isn't her No. It's his No. Oh that hurts, that hurts. Oh how I hate him, he's ruined her life, she's so unhappy, my beautiful daughter.]

The word would have gone round the family: *He doesn't even want the kids to have a dollhouse. Can you imagine?*

The children would have been—well, not disappointed, since they had not as far as she knew been yearning for a dollhouse, but denied; a delightful possibility would have been held for a moment before the eyes of their imaginations and then withdrawn.

The husband: I'm glad you said No to her. [I'm glad she said No to her mother. Even such a small thing, I can see it's hard for her. That bitch, how she tries to keep control—right from the first dinner I had with the parents when the mother was so pissed off because I took more salad without being asked. Why the hell can't she say *No* more often? What the hell stops her? No, no, no—easy to say. Damn middle-class manners. Always phone. Never drop in. Keep the bathroom door closed when you shit. You can't tell what they're feeling half the time. If they feel. Why does she look at me so coldly when I say I am pleased she said No?]

The woman: I'm glad you're glad. [I feel shabby. I feel used. I feel hypocritical. I feel pushed around. His kids mustn't have fun with a dollhouse that comes from their grandmother. I'd like them to have that dollhouse, but I didn't fight for them. Again, I didn't fight for them. Again, I've been a coward.]

Explosion, exploration, shipwreck, mine disaster, epidemic, teaparty, fire, funeral, Victoria Day fireworks, wedding, poisoning, earthquake, New Year's Eve party—all these she remembers playing with her dollhouse and its dolls.

If she had said *No* to her mother, what would she have said to the children? They too had been in the living-room when she was on the phone, had heard *dollhouse*.

The woman: No, dears. It was just a suggestion. Your grandmother was thinking aloud about different things she might get you for Christmas. I didn't think it'd be—suitable. [How many lies is that, in four sentences?]

A daughter: Why do you look sad? [Why does she look sad?]

The woman: Just tired, sweetie. [True, but a lying answer to that question. Did she pick up on that, I wonder. Unfair— they'll be sore at *me* for not letting them have a dollhouse, when all the time . . . . What the hell am I supposed to say if one of them says What is *suitable*? And of course he won't say anything. He'll just smile and let me squirm. But I can't let them see how mad I am at him.]

If she did let them see . . . .

The husband: Why do you make it look as though it's me depriving them of pleasure? [Why is she always against me? Why can't she side with me against her mother? She knows what her mother's up to, why can't she side with me for once? It's her fault.]

The woman: It *is* you depriving them of pleasure. You don't think it's a suitable form of pleasure, I guess. [Why is he angry now? I did what he wanted. I said No to my mother. He's won again, why can't that be enough?]

The husband: You always put me in the wrong in front of them. [Doesn't she have enough on her side? She's the one everybody likes, she's the one who's got a job, she's the one who's being oh-so-perfect about supporting the little family, she's the one who's an artist. She always fixes it so she looks good and I look mean, unco-operative. I give my life over to this damn organization, I live for it, and nobody cares. Nobody sees me as doing anything worthwhile. No validation. She doesn't care. There'd never be a floor swept in this house if it wasn't for me.]

The woman: I don't. And you know I don't. I bend over backwards not to criticize you to them. [Maybe that's where all my back trouble comes from.]

The husband: You're just like your parents. [It's true. It's as if the woman I love disappears, she's swallowed up or vanishes or something, she just isn't there any more. There, that'll shut her up.]

The woman: [The translator breaks down. She has no answer to the awful accusation. True at so many levels, untrue at so many others, the charge paralyzes her vocal cords.]

The husband, continuing: You as a radical? It's not real. Socialism, feminism—they don't go deep in you. The revolutionary party—you were just there on a visit. [She frightens me. She says it all, says it so well, but sometimes I think for her it's just a word game like the others her family plays. At the cottage. The damn cottage.]

The woman: [A second unanswerable accusation, for he is working class and she is middle class. Any defending words would flutter pulverized away before that fact—even though she knows its irrelevance.]

The husband: You never put me first. You never put what I want first. Somebody else is always your priority. [This does not need translation.]

The woman: [She constantly rearranges her everything to accommodate what he proposes, desires, needs. This continual repositioning is, to her, gigantically apparent. Its hopeless hugeness silences her.]

After venting these accusations, the husband might reverse himself.

He might concede: Yes, that dollhouse could be fun for the children. Yet his agreement would be sullen. Like her, he would be unable to conceal his feeling of having been wrongly used. He would steadily remind her (not in front of the children) of his generous tolerance and of her weakness in the workings of this incident. The acid rain of their mutual resentment would contaminate the toy's atmosphere. Bourgeois stupidity.

None of this scenario-writing occurs at the time.

When her mother makes the offer, the woman's inner sensors simply declare, in milliseconds, that it will be ultimately less painful to accept the dollhouse for the children and take the brunt of his hostility than to suffer the resentment, self-hatred, and anger which will metastasize within her if she rejects it.

Better to have than not to have, a bourgeois notion if ever there was one.

Certainly, there is no such thing as a slum dollhouse, a low-rent dollhouse, a dollhouse in need of urban renewal, and in fact the ponderous grandmaternal dollhouse measures out at thirty inches square and twenty high. In the two girls' rooms, because of the configuration of doorways and heating elements and built-in beds, there is no convenient place for it. Also, it is hard to have a Major Toy resident in the room of one, yet available to the other (and her friends). In the hallway? Too narrow. By the foot of the stairs? Too easy to trip over, too dark. Outside on the porch? It will be stolen, or rained on, or shat in by touring cats. Fortnightly rotation from one girl's room to the other's is the eventual solution. The woman must help, each time, because the dollhouse is so heavy.

The girls' father repeatedly says (not in their hearing) *I told you so.*

The girls love the dollhouse. Exuberantly, they rearrange the furniture their grandmother has provided—storebought, not made of plastic, a set for each room—so that each doll has a space exactly the way she or he likes it. They paint bright flowers and potted trees round the base of the building. They trade vigorously with friends to acquire still more small dolls, dishes, pots, pictures, appliances, rugs, bits of string and lace and velours and cork and plastic and ribbon and coloured paper, all of which will be perfect, will make a wonderful something.

These dolls, too, lead a full life.

Every time the grandmother telephones, she asks: Are the children enjoying it?

The younger one complains because the roof is too hard to take off. Besides, when it is on you can't see inside. The woman stores the roof in the closet she shares with her husband. One day it is absent. Eventually she finds it, broken, slung in a corner of their basement storage unit.

Both children disapprove because the dollhouse has no bathroom. The older girl points out that this is just like *Little Women* and *Anne of Green Gables* and *Understood Betsy* and *Little House on the Prairie*, which never tell you how people went to the toilet in the olden days. Taking the best Wilkinson knife from the kitchen, this older daughter cuts a doorway at the end of the central hall. Then she finds scrap plywood and a square of vinyl tile. Using the woman's X-Acto knife, and only cutting herself badly once, she creates the needed room.

(In the second dream, this child is now covered with blisters formed of pain. She is naked, untended, passed over in favour of the greater need of another. Who is that other?)

The younger girl makes a shower curtain out of a bright green plastic bag, and the plastic fixtures carefully chosen at Woolworth's fit neatly. But the bathtub is not satisfactory. To make a drain, the older girl pierces the tub with a heated skewer. The smell of melted plastic suffuses her room. The jagged hole in the tub cannot be effectively stoppered. The woman does not remember how her brother's piping contraption worked.

The girls' father points out to the woman the health hazards of melting plastic, the dangers to young flesh of knives and nails, and the tendency for small sharp breakable objects to stray from the dollhouse, to hurt bare feet or block the vacuum-cleaner. He alone wields the vacuum-cleaner.

The father tells the girls that he admires the work they have done on the dollhouse, their ingenuity.

With time, the younger daughter's interest in Barbies, which do not fit in the dollhouse, intensifies.

The older girl reads.

Somewhere in these months and years, the marriage shatters conclusively.

Sometime after that, the woman and the girls move from the housing co-op into an old rambling house.

A broad hallway on the upper floor, between the girls' rooms, is the perfect site, at last, for the dollhouse. But now the girls are too old for it. The little dwelling sits unplayed with for months on end.

There are kittens, for a while, and they jump in and out of the dollhouse rooms. One goes to sleep in the bathroom and is photographed, with laughter. The kittens, looking important and serious, carry away dolls and bits of cloth and small furnishings in their mouths and drop them here and there. These get swept up, thrown out.

One daughter wants materials for a wall hanging. She takes the livingroom carpet out of the dollhouse; the square of green and brown striped velveteen is a scrap from the grandmother's reupholstering of her sofa, three thousand miles away. Then the younger daughter must make a collage, and rummages through the dollhouse rooms in search of the textural contrasts that the teacher wants.

What a mess, the woman thinks a year or so later.

(Why does that baby in the second dream have that awful sticky pesticide-smelling stuff coming out of its mouth and nose? Can't it cry? Why has it chosen this dreadful way to show its speechlessness? Does it feel that its true voice won't be heard? Is this the younger daughter, less verbal than the rest of the family? Does the touch of her mother's words make her wordlessness worse? Why doesn't the woman know the sex of either of the dream-babies?)

Now the upstairs of the house is to be renovated. The dollhouse, along with everything else from the upper floor, is removed to the basement.

When the fresh rooms are ready, the woman looks forward to reconstituting their furnishings, but the older daughter is fifteen now. She does not want any childhood toys or books or games upstairs. Not that dollhouse. The younger daughter, living with her father, is uninterested.

The dollhouse stays underground.

What will become of the dollhouse? Will it go into the garage sale that the woman and her new partner plan to have, some day? The notion of selling her mother's present makes the woman feel furtive. If her mother were to find out . . . . Hurt, anger.

The woman has a dear friend with a newly-adopted little girl, who in a few years' time will be ready to love a dollhouse. Should the gift be in the hands of strangers?

Why should the thing be kept unused, unenjoyed? The woman's own dollhouse ended up forgotten in the garage. What was the point of that?

Perhaps the woman's ex-husband was right, is right. She is, as always, an object of her mother's use. Her reluctance to dispose of the dollhouse speaks her mother's declaration: *I still own that. It is mine. You and it are mine.*

Or—perhaps after all it is reasonable for an adult daughter to honour a very old mother's wishes. Will her own girls so honour hers? Will she ever have a wish like this?

(All the dream-children in her care are damaged. Count them: one smashed skull; one irreparable skin disease; one respiratory disorder, probably terminal.)

So the dollhouse stays on a storage rack in the basement, by the tent and the sleeping bags and the Coleman stove. Occasionally, when the woman and her new partner are doing chores down there, he says absently *That thing is awfully big, isn't it*, and she says *Yes*.

She is not well yet, but she is better.

Three

"You say *yes* a good deal."

"Yes? I suppose I do."

"And *should. Ought. Supposed to.*"

"And I shouldn't use those?"

"Ah! Again!" Laughter from both therapist and client. "Perhaps we could set up a system of fines? Every time, a nickel?" More laughter.

"I think it would be a good idea if I . . . ."

"Yes. I'm sure that things would have gone better if I had . . . ."

"Even when it's obviously the best thing for me to do . . . ."

(These, and their like, spread through a session.)

"Those expressions of yours—and the *yes*sing. Many people use *yes* like that, to buy their listener's attention. *Favourable* attention. Then they can say what they wanted to in the first place."

"Who is my listener?"

"I want your advice. Not your help, I don't need help. Advice. I'm trying to figure out four dreams I've had. Major dreams."

"Major?"

"I don't usually remember my dreams. Oh, maybe fragments, you know—I don't give them much thought. But these . . . . They all came within a fortnight. Last month. I can't stop thinking about them."

"They moved you?"

A dismissive gesture. "Yes, what do you suppose? I killed a woman, the children were desperately ill, I found a book— of course I was moved. But what do they mean?"

"What do you want from me?"

"Questions. I want you to ask me questions. So I can get a new angle. These dreams—I've talked about them with friends, and they've given me lots of ideas, but—I'm not through yet. I'm not through. I'm sure there's more to them. And I thought that *because* you don't know me, and because of your— training—you might ask unexpected questions."

"Have you considered working with a Jungian?"

Another impatient gesture. "I don't want someone with a preconceived framework for dream interpretation."

"All right. I will play the role you have in mind for me, yes, but you must understand that I'll do and be other things, too. That's inevitable."

"Yes, of course."

"I'm not a vending machine, put in a quarter and an interpretation spits out."

"Of course not. Yes. Here are the dreams."

The manuscript pages, typed double-space, are a pile half an inch high.

"You've written them down."

"I'm a writer."

"But . . . ."

"Believe me, I *know* about editing, bias, concealing. I've been rigorous. I've made myself do it. The dreams *are* on these pages. Fully. Nothing held back. Emphasis as in the original, even if it seems weird, awake."

"Believe *me*. The you-ness of the dreams will be more apparent if you tell them to me."

"Are you refusing to talk about these written dreams with me?"

"She who pays the piper calls the tune, hm? No. I'm not refusing. If you are only comfortable with discussing your written version, that's what we'll do. But you are the dreamer. You are the storyteller. I'll understand much more if you *tell* me your dreams."

"I still think it would be more objective this way."

"With respect—you're not doing literary research now. Not academic criticism."

"Very well, then. I'll begin with the third. It's called The Case of the Skein of Gold and Black."

"*Case?*"

Shrug. "Yes. I'm detecting, sort of." Another shrug, and a short pause. "I'm in Vietnam. I'm kneeling on the earth. A uniform—I'm wearing an American soldier's uniform, and I look like a man. Maybe I even *am* a man, but I don't think so. All over me are weapons. Hunks of metal and plastic. They're tied on my arms and legs and my big pockets are full of them. I can feel the guns against my thighs. The guns press on the stitching of my uniform. The ground—it's cold. Bare. Dark."

"What are you feeling, as you kneel?"

"Big. Armoured. Like a pineapple. The uniform—it's stiff, clumsy. And I feel death not very far away. Some . . . apprehension. I feel alone. But I'm not. I'm looking down at a young Vietnamese woman. She's flat on her back, in front of me."

A deep breath.

"This woman—delicate features. Slight build. Her clothes—a long skirt wrapped tightly. Dusty gold colour. A top in the same fabric. It fits over her small breasts, folds over her shoulders. And I know—I can't see but I know—her hair grows down to her waist. It's hidden mostly, black of course, combed down behind her ears. Small ears. And her eyes—she's glaring at me. Hate, fear."

"And you feel?"

"Excited. Yes, excited. Fast heartbeat. I can hear it. And it speeds up when I see the skein. Wires it might be, or very thin fibres. She's made it, I know."

"A skein?"

"Well—if you took a bundle of your mother's old-fashioned hairpins, the kind like tiny croquet-hoops with crinkles in them, and if they were much longer, the length of your arm . . . . The skein's lying next to her, on the ground."

"And you feel . . . ?"

"Don't you ever ask anything else? I *want* that skein. It's black, and gold, mixed and shining. What is it? What is it for? I want to take those fibres in my hand, so I reach out, I lean over the woman and reach for her skein."

A pause. A sigh.

"The Vietnamese woman—she fights me. *Fights.* She's so small and thin, but she struggles and pushes, she won't let me at the skein. I was so surprised, in the dream! She looked so—there didn't seem to be much to her. Her arms were so thin."

Speaking faster now. "Those skinny arms—she reaches up and she presses her two forefingers against my two temples. My God, the pain! Like darning-needles going into my head."

"And you feel . . . ?"

"Oh shock, shock. From her! The last thing I expected. It hurt so much I stopped reaching for the skein. I wanted to hold my poor head. Oh, I hurt so! And my knees trembled. I was all weak and frightened, almost driven back."

The eyes are closed now.

"Almost?"

"I went into a rage. I attacked her. I'm big, I'm strong, I'm healthy and vigorous and North American, I put my hands round her neck and I squeeze till I feel the bones crunch and the throat collapse into itself. I wring that woman's neck. It's easy."

The eyes open. "And I feel? Good. Happy. I enjoyed it. I felt the anger boiling all through me, rage from toes to ears, and I killed her. I *wanted* that treasure, so badly." Sigh. "So. What do you think it means?"

"Sometimes I think there is nothing so hindering as an active intelligence. The way you're going about this—characteristic, of course, from what I've seen of you."

"How so?"

"Ingenious. Strenuous. Cerebral."

"I told you—my aim is to understand this dream. And the other three."

"That won't happen, if you use your intellect only."

"You think I should feel more?"

"Nickel, please . . . . The feelings *in* the dreams, *about* the dreams. Those are at least as important as anyone's ideas about them."

"But they *hurt*, dammit. I don't want to feel them again, why should I?" Shifting in the chair. "Look at old people—all worn out, tired from decades of feeling. They don't care about anything much. They can't. Those dream feelings—just thinking about them makes me tired."

"Emotional exhaustion isn't the goal. And you're far from

old. But—what you call the symbols of the dream, the design,
the message—let's come *to* them. Why do you want to start
with them?"

"This isn't what I wanted."

"I told you that I could not only ask questions."

"This isn't what I had in mind."

"I've done some drawings. Sort of. Collages, really. Of the
dreams."

"You've brought them?"

"One. The others aren't finished yet. It's an attempt at a visual
approach. To meaning."

Something like a giant seed-pod explodes in pencil, felt-pen,
watercolour on the white sheet. At the outer limits of the burst,
either directly on the paper or pasted on multi-coloured paper
scraps, are quotations, lines of poetry, film titles, names of
painters, a tiny musical stave with a bar or two, dictionary defi-
nitions, questions, equations, notes on symbols, a couple of
games of Hangman.

The centre is the skein. The technique: using a dispenser with
a slender opening, trail strings of glue over and over the page,
not scrawling and messy but carefully ordered and twined. Dust
these with thousands of minute round glass beads, two-thirds
of them black, one-third gold. Let dry. Shake off excess.

Towards the lower left of the sheet are attached a pair of artificial nails, long, tapered to needle points. They emit zigzags of
purple felt-pen pain. Towards the upper right is a colour photo
of a hand grenade, outlined in scarlet.

"I thought of framing them, when they're done. Putting them
up, in the dining-room maybe. For this one—I thought of
braiding together some khaki and some gold lamé strips and
trailing them off the edge, here. To get—I don't know. Dimen-
sion. I wish I could draw better. There should be more curves,
more curving out, off the page. I wish I could do that," with
the voice breaking.

"In your line of work, you must see a lot of tears. Do they get boring?"

"Sometimes they just fall gently out. Like a full container that slops over a bit. But some—they drive out of the eyes as if the tears behind were shooting at them. All rushing to make way for the new ones forming at the root."

"The root."

"Why do you ask?"

"In the dream, what did you want to do with the skein?"

"To make something with it."

"What had the Vietnamese woman done?"

"She'd braided it into her hair for some—rite, religious ceremony maybe. Some traditional thing."

"An ornamental use, then."

"Not in the useless sense."

"And your use would be . . . ?"

Long pause. "I just wanted to hold that beautiful stuff in my hands. If I could have, I would have known what to make with it. How to work with it."

"Your use would be individual, not traditional. Innovative?"

"No, too trendy. But yes, I would do something not done before. It was so beautiful in itself—you couldn't help but make something beautiful with it."

"*You?*"

"I."

"How do you feel, that you couldn't make anything?"

"Frustrated, in the dream. Now—sad. I didn't even get to touch it, because her fingers came up at my head. If only I'd asked. I should have asked. But that's stupid. Soldiers don't ask permission. Not of frail tiny women lying on the ground in front of them."

"The Vietnamese woman. Clearly, she is The Feminine."

"Clearly?"

"My God, haven't I described her in enough detail? Look.

A victim. Passive. Beautiful, and beautifully dressed. Frightened. Poisonous—those needle fingers shot poison into my head. A maker—she made that skein, textiles, classic feminine product. Magical. Who has fingernails like that? She made me go out of my mind, go wild and kill. Dark-skinned, not my race. In my culture, that means alien, dangerous. Evil maybe. And she's been invaded, penetrated, dammit! That's why I'm in her country. I'm an invading solder. *And* she's killed. The ultimate feminine experience."

"And you feel?"

"I was Rambo, I was an American in Vietnam, how blatant can you get in a dream, and I killed the feminine. How the hell do you suppose I feel? I enjoyed killing, remember, in the dream?"

"Did you love her?"

"I wanted her treasure. I was enraged when she wouldn't give it to me. I didn't decide—I just acted. To get her treasure, I strangled her."

"Did you love her?"

"It was rape. See the picture? The small woman is flat on her back on the ground. The burly soldier *leans* over her to rip away what she's willing to die for. He kills her because she won't give him what he wants, won't consent."

"Did you love her?"

"I envied her. Is that love? That small beauty. Women like me feel bad around it. It shows us up. The little feet, waists. Us—big solid husky hearty women—blunderers. Oxen. Lumps."

"You feel unfeminine?"

"Look—in that dream I don't even know for certain if I'm a woman or a man. In two of the others, I don't know if the babies are boys or girls. I know I ought to know, but I don't know. But that woman—she could only be female."

"What do you feel?"

"Angry. You see? I've laid the blame on *her*. She made me angry. She made me senselessly violent. To get her vitality, I killed her. To save the village, destroy it. To save Vietnam from

Communism, bomb it back to the Stone Age."

"If everyone in a dream is in some way the dreamer—then who is this woman in you?"

Quick and cool, "My femininity. My creativity. At the least, she's in charge of some part of my creativity."

"If she was only passive, why did she fight so bravely, even though she must have known she couldn't defeat you? Surely her hatred, her courage, were very strong? If she was only a victim, why was she so determined? Why was she so intelligent? Yes, she was, she targeted your most vulnerable point, hm? If she was so weak, how come she hurt you so much you had to stop trying to get her treasure?"

"If I turned it around . . . ."

"If you turned what around?"

"If I turned the dream of the Vietnamese woman around . . . ."

"Penny for your thoughts."

"Always money terms! If I turned it around. *If I were her.* If I were all those things I first said of her, plus all those things you just said. And if it were me defending myself. Fighting to the death. But—did I die, then?"

"Do you feel dead?"

Four

We looked at each other, two women in our odd respective roles, and we laughed.

I liked that therapist. She was direct and clear and she did not behave as if the person in the chair opposite were a dolt, nor did she speak in that flat tone that so many professionals develop. Always her voice was lively, engaged. She took an interest in the life that came before her view, and not just because that was her job. I think she must be a good friend to her friends. I liked her office, too. The flowers were silk and paper (clients' allergies), but vibrant against the pale walls. When I was there, late on winter afternoons, the woven lampshade cast inexact patterns of yellow and grey. She had hung a set of chimes just by the window. They were made of shells, and gave off a melody frail as the scent of arbutus bark.

While I was seeing her, I also powered through books and articles on dream interpretation. Skimming contents and abstracts and indices, I sought blankets, cracked skulls, dying babies, gold and black fibres, strangling, bodily sores, exudations from the mouth, uncertainty about gender, underground passages, mothers and daughters, soldiers, head wounds, skin colour, poisoned needles, islands, absence of men from women's dreams . . . .

Sometimes she and I discussed these sources, picking up a insight from here, binding it to a thought from there . . . .

But after all and after all, the words used by even the best of those people, whether black on the page or spoken in attractive offices, sound *thin*. Like mediocre poetry, they are inexact, partial; or they are like the dubbing of foreign films, when a character speaks passionately for twenty-one seconds and the subtitle reads "I told you so." True . . . but the context is absent. Whole truth is lost in translation.

However, the questions she threw at me, even when they felt mis-aimed, off-centre, *were* useful, because in them she showed me herself. Quirky, insistent, sharp, affectionate, she looked at *me*, and I saw her seeing me, so I saw more.

A time came, and it was the same time, when I stopped seeing her and I stopped reading. I was through.

Although I am nearly half a century old, I am sometimes unable to decide or to speak because I am afraid of angry disapproval: my mother's, my father's, my husband's. In my marriage, fear made me unable to speak truly for myself, unable to make my case—and a strong case it was.

Many times I have tried to visualize this fear, to write scenarios. *If I knew what I feared, I could deal with it . . . .* However, I never get very far with these imaginings. *He would be angry*

at me. *She would be angry at me. He would show that he disapproved.*
I stick there. Fear of rejection: a subtitle. Yet I can't be more
precise. The only thing clear is that *I would be unable to speak.*
    This cowardice, most painfully experienced in my relations
with my former husband and my always mother (occasionally in other areas of my life), appears to be chronic. I do not
believe I will ever overcome it. Rather, I see myself as like a
diabetic or arthritic person. Such people, and I, are not bad or
weak. We are disabled. Every day the diabetic shoots up. Every
day the arthritic eats the pills. Every day, both know that if they
don't inject or eat, disaster will be right there with them. Both
know the names of their disorders, know how the diseases work
in their inner systems. But who knows *why* anyone contracts
diabetes? arthritis? cowardice?
    The germ of my disorder may lie in the body of my grand-
mother, dead of puerperal fever a few days after she gave birth
to my mother. Motherless, then wickedly stepmothered, my
mother came to motherhood herself with a huge passionate
hunger. I was *so* wanted, *so* badly wanted, *so* important to her,
so valuable, *so* wonderful . . . any child born to meet such a want
would find it hard to sustain herself as herself. I shoot up and
eat my pills. Working with those black and gold fibres that are
my mother's hair, I make things.
    In The Case of the Book that Brought Happiness, I walk with
my younger daughter, Theresa, on a high hill in a green sunlit
city. Behind us, beyond the city and to the west, the country
turns to mountains, but our prospect is southeast and over the
whole metropolis. This city is very large, millions of people,
and is built on broad slopes that flow before us in a great rolling expanse down to the glittering river in the distance. The
curving water divides the vistas of streets, houses, office towers,
factories. Many of the city's buildings are pastel, or white, and
the river is blue, yet this is not a Mediterranean city. This is
my North America, familiar and beautiful and loved. The light,
the high airiness, the sense of being one of two among a great
population, the quiet neighbourhood—all these make me
happy.

Theresa and I are looking for a certain apartment building. We know it's nearby, so we are not anxious or fretting, just happily going together along these sunny streets with their tall leafy chestnut trees. Because of the steep terrain here, small retaining walls and embankments of whitewashed stone make the descending street levels into terraces. Bright small flowers grow round the stones. Theresa climbs up and down; she runs ahead of me to check street names; she comes running, jumping, calling; she laughs, and giggles, and points out dogs on windowsills and odd marks on the sidewalk and roses in the gardens.

When we find the building and get into the apartment and then into the livingroom, we will find the wonderful book. Imagining that book makes both of us happy. The book is big, square, hard-backed, printed on specially thin paper because of its many pages. Oh, we will be able to read this book for a long long time! As we walk, we picture the book lying open on the table, by the window. We see tree leaves and book leaves flutter in the warm bright air. We hear the crisp rustle of the pages. We will get the book and sit together on one of these sunny lawns, reading more, and reading more.

Now Theresa and I come to a building of pale grey stone at the corner of a block. Fresh young ivy is spreading over it, the tender leaves intensely green and translucent. Low on one wall of this building is a relief map of the whole neighbourhood, made of some dark metal with the streets picked out in bright brass. Now we will surely find the building and the book! We look at the neat shining letters. At once, the map reveals the street we want; it's only a block away.

Delighted, Theresa and I take hands. Hers is young and warm and fits perfectly in the curve of mine. We walk happily over the sunlit city hill to find our story.